www.**deepakdalal**.com

Also on FACEBOOK

A VIKRAMADITYA STORY
DEEPAK DALAL

THE SNOW LEOPARD *Adventure*

DEEPAK DALAL

Silverfish
in association with
Westland Ltd

Grey Oak Publishers
2nd Floor, Prestige Omega, No. 104 EPIP Zone, Whitefield
Bangalore 560066
www.greyoak.in

westland ltd
61, Silverline Building, Alapakkam Main Road, Maduravoyal, Chennai 600 095
No. 38/10 (New No.5), Raghava Nagar, New Timber Yard Layout, Bangalore 560 026
23/181, Anand Nagar, Nehru Road, Santacruz East, Mumbai 400 055
93, 1st Floor, Sham Lal Road, Daryaganj, New Delhi 110 002
www.westlandbooks.in

First published by Tarini Publishing, 2000

The Snow Leopard Adventure is published by Silverfish, an imprint of Grey Oak Publishers, in association with westland ltd 2013.

10 9 8 7 6 5 4 3 2 1

ISBN 978-93-82618-45-4

Cover photograph: Dhritiman Mukherjee
Cover Design: Sourabh Choudhary
Title page illustration: Anusha Menon
Original illustrations: Shailesh Sonawane
Illustrations Redrawn: Yogendra Joshi, Nagendra K, Pradnya Apte
Map - Geographical inputs: Dr. Sanjeev Nalawade
Map - Illustration: Dr. Sanjeev Nalawade
Typesetting: Aditi Deo, Damini Rawal

Printed by HT Media Ltd., Noida

Acknowledgements

I had spoken to Joanna when I planned to write a book based in Ladakh. I explained to her that I wanted to do a story on the snow leopard because it was an animal that fascinated me. "No problem," she told me. "Get in touch with my husband, Raghu. He has been studying snow leopards for years." I did, and Raghu invited me on his annual snow leopard expedition. This book is a result of that expedition.

Prelude

The following is the text of a report handed to Vikram just before he left Leh on the snow leopard expedition.

Investigation of the Tiger Bone - Shahtoosh Trade in Ladakh

A report prepared by the Wildlife Society of India

The high altitude plateaus of Tibet are the home of the Tibetan antelope or the Chiru as it is locally known. Once, the Chirus, in many hundreds of thousands, roamed the Changthang*, but in recent times their numbers have been dramatically reduced.

The dense undercoat of the Chiru (called shahtoosh) protects it from the extreme weather conditions of the Changthang. Unfortunately for the antelope, the wool that is spun from its down hair is considered the finest in the world. Shahtoosh is the ultimate in wool and is often referred to as the 'king wool'. It is very fine and exceptionally soft and warm. The wool is woven into luxurious shawls that are prized the world over.

In the past, hunting and the demand for shahtoosh were minimal, and had little impact on the vast herds of Chiru. However, demand from the fashion industry has dramatically pushed up the value of the wool and killing of the animals has since become an extremely profitable venture.

The herds which roamed the Changthang have been

* Tibetan word, meaning northern plain

decimated and China has recently banned the killing of ntelopes. Though the trade in shahtoosh has been banned worldwide, it still persists. The Wildlife Society of India (WSI) has been investigating this illegal practice and has lately uncovered chilling facts about the trade.

A barter system exists along the border of Ladakh and Tibet, where shahtoosh wool is exchanged for tiger bones. Bones of tigers killed in the game sanctuaries of India are collected and brought to Leh, in Ladakh. The bones are then handed over to the nomadic Changpa people who carry them on the backs of yaks, across remote Himalayan passes, into Tibet. The nomads hand over the bones to their Chinese counterparts and collect the wool in exchange, which they bring back into India.

We have established that an organised gang conducts the entire operation. They ensure that the shahtoosh reaches the city of Srinagar in Kashmir where it is woven into shawls and scarves. The shawls are then smuggled out of India and sold to wealthy clients across the world for fabulous sums of money.

Besides spurring the slaughter of the antelope, this trade also threatens the survival of the Indian tiger. It was actually our investigation into the tiger bone trade that revealed these alarming facts. Ever since we discovered this distressing development, the WSI has directed all its energies towards this case and recently we have achieved a significant breakthrough.

We now know that the leader of the international gang involved in the shahtoosh trade is a gentleman named Akira Singh. Mr. Akira Singh was born in Hong Kong to a Japanese mother and an Indian father and is fluent in Japanese, Chinese and Hindi. Despite his half-Indian lineage, his looks are decidedly Japanese and he enters India posing as a Japanese tourist. After arranging tiger bone shipments from Delhi, he travels to Leh and oversees the smuggling operation into Tibet. He transports the shahtoosh he obtains as barter to Srinagar where shawls and scarves are woven. He organises the smuggling of these illegal items out of India and sells them to a contact in Hong Kong who arranges for their worldwide distribution.

WSI has information that Mr. Akira Singh is currently in Ladakh. A recent photograph of his is enclosed with this report. If anyone sees this man or has information regarding him please contact WSI immediately.

Vikram's Diary

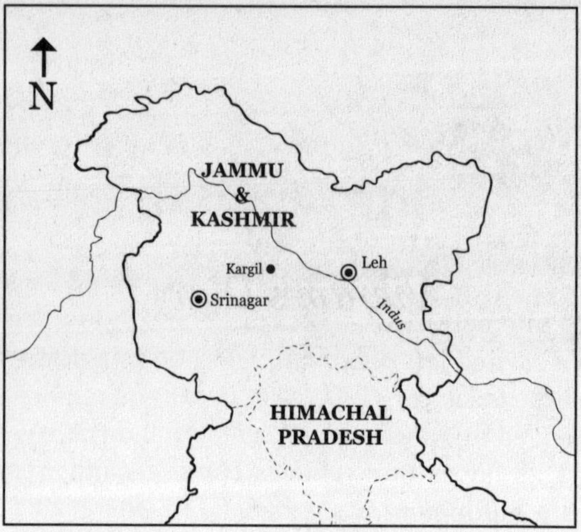
N
JAMMU
&
KASHMIR
Kargil
Leh
Srinagar
Indus
HIMACHAL
PRADESH

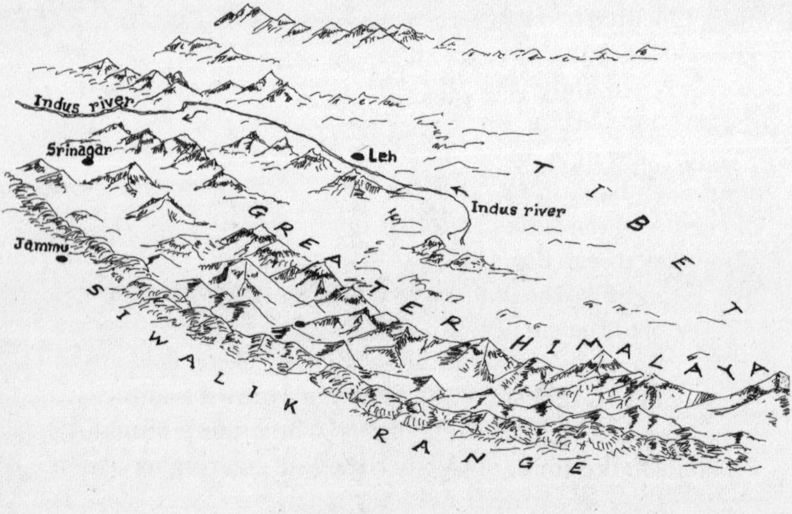
Indus river
Srinagar
Leh
TIBET
Indus river
GREATER HIMALAYA
Jammu
SIWALIK RANGE

Day 1

About 15 kilometres from Leh, just short of Phyang village, our jeeps turned left off the highway on to a dirt track. We followed the track through green fields and apple orchards, until it ended at a footbridge that spanned the river Indus. This was as far as our vehicles could go and we alighted here. Our equipment was loaded on the backs of tiny Ladakhi ponies and mules.

Aware that I was crossing a river of great historical and geographical significance, I paused on the footbridge to gaze down at it. "*Indu Mata*" I had been told, mother of India. I stood there in awe, trying humbly to contemplate its grandeur. The river was wide here and its grey waters, which had originated in neighbouring Tibet, flashed past at a brisk speed under the bridge.

The first part of the trek was hot, sweaty and dusty. The sun was high above us and we were walking through a huge sandy plain towards the base of the mountains. On the banks of the Indus I spotted fields of barley and stands of poplar trees. But this was the only visible greenery. Everywhere else the landscape was so stark and barren that it resembled the surface of the moon. The endless plain we walked along was remarkable for its lack of plant life, and the mountains that surrounded us were brown and rocky.

Ladakh is a high altitude desert. The mighty Himalaya which lie to the south of us block the rain-bearing monsoon clouds. They say it does not rain much here. But there is plenty of water in Ladakh. The mighty Indus is unstoppable. It flows throughout the year and so do several other streams and rivers which are fed by meltwater from glaciers and snow capped peaks.

Our group, like most trekking parties, had spread itself out. Those who preferred to walk fast had gone on ahead, while those who chose to linger and admire the barren wilderness had fallen behind. The sun blazed down from a crystal blue sky. We had peeled off our warm clothes and stuffed them in our backpacks. Little Tsering, dressed in a white T-shirt, walked beside me. Aditya was way up in front, chatting with the ladies in our group.

There are eleven of us including little Tsering. We are quite an international team. From the US, Singapore, the UK, Australia, Tibet and India – we have all come together. Our quest is the animal called the snow leopard. Dr. Raghu Raman is our expedition leader. Our task is to aid him in his studies of this mysterious and mystical animal often referred to as the 'grey ghost' of the Himalaya.

I am excited and so is Aditya. We are finally on our way. We have both decided to put our troubles behind us and enjoy this trip. The elusive snow leopard...are we going to find it? Raghu is not sure but both Aditya and I are convinced we will. We are rivals – who will find the leopard first? Aditya is confident he will. I think otherwise.

We followed the river Indus, walking above it along an elevated plain. After a long, exhausting hour we halted to regroup and collect our breath. There was a river confluence where we broke our journey. Blue water surged out from the mountains, tumbling downhill and mingling with the grey currents of the Indus.

My mind boggled at the stark scenery about us. It was a fantastic wilderness, so desolate and so strange that I felt threatened by it. Crumbling peaks sprouted amidst vast barren plateaus. Visibility was perfect and we could see for miles, but there was no sign of human habitation. The thundering presence of water seemed at odds with the desert like landscape around us. The only glimmer of life was a pair of black ravens hovering far below, just above the waters of the Indus.

Pointing to the blue waters that flowed into the Indus, Raghu informed us that they belonged to a river called the Rumbak. We were now going to turn away from the Indus and enter the mountains. The river Rumbak presented us a gateway, Raghu said. Its watercourse was the easiest route into the mountains.

A serious uphill climb began now. The river gorge was like a twisting channel and it undulated forever upwards. The pleasant sound of water accompanied us as we toiled forward. The river had the habit of swinging from wall to wall and we were often forced to wade its freezing waters over cold, slippery stones. Water crossings were repeated several times, much to our annoyance and discomfort.

Zinchin is the tiniest village I have ever seen. It consists of only two long, flat-roofed dwellings. Tall poplar trees suddenly appeared in the river valley. A string of prayer flags announced human habitation. Then came the pair of lonely houses and the fields. We stopped for a while to enjoy the coolness beneath the trees.

The village soon vanished behind a curve in the river. Greenery faded and barren wastes swallowed us once again. Crumbling rock towered steeply around as we trudged wearily upwards. There is far less oxygen in the air at 13,000 feet than at sea level. We had to stop often to gather our breath, panting heavily as our oxygen-starved lungs strained at the rarefied air around us. Thank God we were not carrying our rucksacks! The going would have been infinitely more difficult if we were bent double under their load. The ponies are a blessing and thanks to them, all we need carry is a small daypack on our backs.

Our first campsite is a flattened section of land hemmed in on all sides by sharply rising mountains. Working as a team we quickly set up camp. Six brightly coloured tents were pitched side by side. Tsering and I were assigned a blue, dome shaped tent. The sun was sinking in the western sky and I hurriedly unpacked and arranged my belongings inside the tent while there was light.

Three additional tents were set up beside our sleeping tents. One is a huge, green dining tent which can seat all the members of our expedition. Another tent is the kitchen. The third is what we call the 'loo' tent. It is a tall, rectangular tent pitched over a hole in the ground that serves as a commode. This tent, of course, is located some distance away from the others.

There was a scramble for binoculars when Raghu pointed at a nearby mountain and exclaimed, "Bharal...blue sheep!" The mountain was impossibly high and somewhere near its top we spotted four shadows. The animals I saw certainly did not look like sheep and neither were they blue. Bundled in our jackets (the evening chill had set in), we all stood there, dutifully staring at the oddly named animals. Unlike any sheep I have seen they possessed no fleecy wool. They were grey and stood much taller than domestic sheep. I think their local name 'bharal' sounds far more appropriate to me.

Blue sheep are an important prey species of the snow leopard, Raghu informed us. There is always a possibility of spotting a leopard when you see bharal. My veins tingled as I scanned the mountains. But all I saw were barren slopes.

Stars were appearing in the sky when the camp boys called us in for dinner. Flickering kerosene lanterns illuminated the steaming food. It was warm and cheerful inside the tent. We laughed and chatted as we ate. The meal brought all the members of our expedition together and gave us the opportunity to acquaint ourselves with each other.

Our team members are:

Dr. Raghu Raman: Expedition leader and dedicated wildlife scientist. Bearded gentleman who wears a green hat at all times. Medium build, yet endowed with exceptional stamina. Irritable but possesses a wonderful heart.

Tina Kuruvilla: Indian lady from Kerala. Age around 30 years. Raghu's second-in-command. Dark complexioned and athletic. Keen, enthusiastic wildlife researcher. Fun loving but studious. Always concerned about everybody else and constantly worried about the smooth functioning of the camp.

Julia and Caroline Austin: From the US of A. Julia is the mother and Caroline the daughter. Caroline must be in her late teens, 18 or 19 years old. She is tall, fair-skinned, dark-haired and quite beautiful. Her beauty, however, is marred by a permanent pout on her face. Julia, the mother, is fair-skinned but there is a strong Asian hint to her features. Tina says Julia's father was from India. Julia and Caroline are the strangest couple in our group. Julia at least laughs and talks, but Caroline does not. I wonder whether she ever wanted to come on this expedition. Maybe her mother dragged her along.

Kathy and Richard Smith: British couple in their late forties. Richard is a director of a pharmaceutical company and Kathy is a doctor. They live in London and are both wildlife lovers. Kathy identifies each bird we see and tells us everything about it. Richard too is a fountain of knowledge. He and Raghu have endless discussions on wildlife management in the Himalaya.

Yuan Lee: Computer engineer from Singapore. Approximately 40 years old. Medium build, slightly taller than Raghu. Serious nature. Smiles at all our jokes, but rarely cracks any himself. Avid outdoor man. Loves the mountains and this is his third trip to the Himalaya.

Roger Allen: Australian. 25 years old. Tall, strapping man. This is his first visit to India and the Himalayas. Manager of a supermarket in Sydney. Loves to talk and jest. Fit, strong outdoor man.

Tsering Ringmo: Young, reincarnated lama. Less than ten years old and cannot speak Hindi or English. Impish smile and soulful eyes that endear him to everybody. Last-moment, surprise addition to the expedition.

Vikram Singh and Aditya Khan: We are the only schoolboys and the youngest members of the expedition after Tsering.

Our support team:

Camp boys: Tashi and Tsewang. Young Ladakhi brothers.

Cooks: Wangchuk and Sonam.

Horseman: Karma.

We sat on stools outside the tent after dinner. A half-moon shone down on us and the sky was an inverted bowl of sparkling stars. There wasn't much talk between us. We sat together silently observing the cold, moonlit mountains. It had been a long, tiring day and we trickled away one by one, returning to our tents. I fell asleep the moment my head touched my pillow.

Day 2

Although the day did not start too well, it turned out to be quite an eventful one. Caroline and her mother Julia were not present at the dining tent for breakfast. They turned up much later, when most of us had completed our meal and returned to our tents. Roger, Aditya, Tsering and myself had lingered, chatting and enjoying extra cups of coffee. We greeted them when they finally did show up. Mrs. Austin smiled at us but Caroline refused to look in our direction. Her face was red and her eyes were swollen as if she had been crying.

It was only later that I found out what the matter was. The story was not very pleasant. When Caroline visited the 'loo' tent in the morning she overbalanced and fell into the commode. We had all been using the tent so the pit beneath her was not empty. A horror stricken and nauseated Caroline had rushed out. The only water available to cleanse herself with was the river. But the morning temperature of the river water is just a degree or two above freezing. Caroline had plunged in regardless. I can imagine the state in which her mother, who had run behind her had found her: weeping, sickened, numbed and revolted with herself. Poor girl, this is an experience I would not wish on anybody.

Our morning departure was held up because of this unfortunate incident. While we were waiting Raghu divided us into two groups. Tsering and I were in Tina's group (along with Yuan Lee, Kathy Smith and a tearful and sulky Caroline). Aditya was assigned to Raghu's team.

The idea behind splitting us into groups, Tina told us,

was to cover as much area as possible. We were to look for snow leopard sign in the mountains behind the camp; the others had been allotted an area on the far side of the river. Finding or sighting a snow leopard is not easy. According to Tina and Raghu it is a distinctly low possibility. This elusiveness of the animal presents a problem to researchers. How can you study an animal if you cannot find it? You have to search for evidence of its presence, Tina told me. Our task today is to find, catalogue and study all evidence of its sign.

The mountain we climbed was eroding beneath our feet. With every step we dislodged stones and clouds of powdered rock. I wondered whether Tina was testing us, because she led us along treacherous tracks barely a foot across, where a single missed step could result in a fall. She told us to kick hard at every stride and to dig deep for purchase on the slippery, gravel-crusted mountainside. There were times when I held my breath and prayed. Tsering never hesitated while crossing the dangerous sections, even Kathy and Yuan had no problems, but both Caroline and I would inch forward slowly and hesitatingly. I suspect that her legs quaked and shivered as much as mine.

We climbed steadily upwards and the camp soon shrank to a stain of colourful specks way below us. Up here, in the high reaches, we found plenty of snow leopard sign. We, of course, would all have walked blissfully past the signs if it weren't for Tina. She seemed to possess an incredibly sensitive snout, especially tuned to sniff evidence of a leopard. She detected invisible paths which the animals had walked along, and on these paths she pointed out leopard scrapes near the rubble-covered tracks. Like magnetised search beams her eyes would sift out leopard scat (excretions). Leopard scats are palm sized: black if fresh, and grey if old. Each scat was collected with a pair of tweezers and carefully packed in brown paper bags. The exact location where the scat was picked up was noted on a label and stuck on the bags. The scats would be taken back to Tina and Raghu's study centre at Dehradun and their analysis would yield detailed information on the snow leopard's diet.

Tina was particularly excited by a fresh specimen of scat that she found. It was still moist. According to her, it had been excreted just a few hours earlier. A leopard had passed this way the previous night!

We were standing below an abruptly ascending wall of rock. Tina thought that the leopard had climbed the wall. To my dismay she seemed keenly interested in following the animal. She, Kathy and Yuan studied the wall and decided that there was a way up. They were eager to continue and search for the leopard. Caroline and I showed reluctance. Little Tsering didn't seem to mind either way.

The wall was climbable but it was going to be tough. My legs would turn to jelly again. Caroline solved my problem by refusing to go any further. She had followed all morning without protest. She had handled the intricate, dangerous sections without a murmur – but the wall ahead was too much. She was not going to attempt it.

The others were determined to go ahead and so Tina split our group. She, Kathy and Yuan would ascend the wall. For the rest of us she chose a rocky crest, a considerable distance to our right. There was a wonderful view from the crest, she said. She wanted Caroline, Tsering and me to go there and survey the surrounding slopes for sheep (and leopard if we were lucky). It was around eleven then. They would join us at the crest in an hour's time.

The crest was roughly a 20-minute hike. There was no Tina to push us and so the three of us walked leisurely. The view from up here was grand. To one side, our mountain towered above us, reaching for the sky. On the other side, it plunged precipitously downwards. The Rumbak river, which we had followed from the Indus, was a tiny thread far beneath us. The valley it had cut for itself was clearly defined. My eyes followed it, from its lower reaches which we had toiled along, up past our brightly coloured tents, till it disappeared behind a fold in the mountains.

Down in the valleys our range of vision had been restricted by the mountains soaring above us. But our climb had drawn us out of the valleys, and now from the elevated vantage point we stood at we could see snow-capped peaks glistening in the morning sun. Raghu had said that the ice on some of the peaks was permanent. The long, crazily shaped rivers of ice that adorned some of the mountains were glaciers. I knew that one of the dazzling summits belonged to Stok Kangri (the most prominent peak visible from Leh), but I couldn't tell which one it was. I felt a delightful shiver of excitement as I gazed at the frozen expanse. We would soon be camping up there, below the jumble of gleaming glaciers.

Tsering pointed across to the slopes opposite. Far in the distance, like tiny multi-coloured bugs, we could see Raghu's group. They were sitting under a huge rock overhang halfway up a purple coloured mountain. Caroline showed little interest in Raghu's group despite the fact that her mother was one of those 'bugs'. The grandeur of the scenery appeared to have no effect on her at all. She preferred instead to stare at the ground and kick distractedly at the loose gravel at her feet.

Caroline lagged behind when we resumed walking. After a while Tsering and I heard rumblings from behind. She was mumbling and muttering to herself and her tone was not particularly pleasant. Not surprisingly, when we were about halfway to the crest, Caroline protested that she was tired and did not want to walk any further. Tsering, with his innocent, childish smile insisted on taking her pack. The little lama's selfless gesture persuaded Caroline to keep going a little longer. But five minutes later we heard rumblings once again. While she grumbled I spied a snow leopard scat, the very first that I had spotted on my own.

It was when I proudly reached down to pick it up that Caroline erupted. Her simmering anger suddenly flared and hot words spewed from her like fiery lava.

"Shit!" she exclaimed. "Is that what this entire trip is about?!" Her chin trembled. "I fall into it in the morning and then I spend the rest of the day collecting it!" Her voice was breaking and I knew that tears were not far away. "Why did I ever allow myself to come to this awful place? These mountains disgust me, the food is unbearable and camp life stinks!"

Caroline crumpled to the track and buried her face in her hands. Shocked at the girl's outburst I stared bemusedly at her. When I looked helplessly at Tsering he winked and held his hands over his mouth, holding back a giggle.

Though I am comfortable with girls, there are some who intimidate me. Caroline is one of them. Aditya had been publicly rebuked when he had tried to chat her up and so had Roger. After witnessing the response they got, I hadn't even made an attempt. Now, on a mountainside 15,000 feet above sea level, I had the same standoffish girl sobbing bitterly by my side. Her mother, who was the only one who could handle her, was many kilometres away. The women in my team, Tina and Kathy, who might have eased the situation, were not here. Thoroughly dumbfounded I gazed at Caroline's hunched body.

I think my presence must have infuriated Caroline. Sobbing like an infant in front of a stranger must be humiliating. After a couple of minutes of hysterical crying she calmed down and turned on me with a furious expression. She was quite a sight to behold. Her fair skin was hidden behind a veil of grime, and her face was streaked with teary trails. In the sunlight I saw that her hair was not entirely black, it had a tinge of golden brown. Her blue eyes glittered like glacial ice.

"What are you staring at?!" she shrieked. "Can't you people leave me alone?! Go away! Get away from me! I want

to be left alone!" Her voice had a dangerous edge to it.

I stood there not saying a word.

Tsering giggled behind me.

That did it! Caroline turned and stomped away from us. When I made an attempt to follow, she turned and fixed me with a withering glare. She then spun around and ran blindly away from us.

"Stop!" I yelled.

Caroline was rushing along a cliff edge. What she was doing was absolutely crazy. The mountainside demanded care and extreme caution; it was not a place to dash heedlessly along. I shouted at her to stop, but my cries only spurred her on.

The slope we were walking on was uneven and sharp. There were many rocky outcrops on the mountainside, and when Caroline stormed away, she strode along the firm base of one such outcrop. Concerned only about getting away from us the girl paid scant attention to where she placed her feet. No one walks blindly on mountain slopes, but Caroline did, and she instantly paid the penalty.

I didn't see what exactly happened because I was looking down at the rock as I ran. I heard a scream and when I looked up I saw a pair of hands grabbing desperately at the edge of the outcrop. I was not far behind Caroline and scarcely a few seconds must have elapsed between her falling and my flinging myself to the ground and locking my fingers around her wrists. I had barely grasped them when her scrabbling fingers slipped and her entire weight was suddenly transferred onto me. I was dragged forward and my chest hit the rock with a thud.

We were both stuck, she dangling from my hands and I pressed against the cliff edge, pinned down by her weight. Caroline is three inches taller than my 5 feet 7 inches and also heavier than me (65 kg. to my 60, she told me later). I could feel myself being pulled towards the edge. Disaster appeared to be a certainty, but Tsering intervened, saving us by clinging to my thighs and adding his weight to mine.

Now, on reflection, I don't think any of us would have died if we had gone over. The cliff we clung to was not a large one and the fall was only ten metres. But the area at the base of the cliff was not flat, it sloped downwards at an alarming angle. The injuries we might have sustained could have been serious and there most definitely would have been a few broken bones.

My breath came in rapid gulps and sweat must have flowed from my every pore. Yet, even though I was terrified, a part of my mind admired the vista spread before me. My position at the edge of the cliff presented me a splendid view. I could see the river valley below and the mountain slopes opposite. I spotted coloured specks in the distance – our camp mates. I wondered if they could see us.

I am ashamed to admit that I lost control of myself up there. My hands shook and my chest hurt terribly. My heart thudded faster than an express train and my senses swam about me. I kept telling myself that there was no reason to panic and that nobody would go over. I had no idea then that I was speaking my thoughts aloud (Caroline and Tsering informed me later). I told myself that we had to only wait it out. Somebody would come...Tina and Kathy would return soon and untangle us.

Luckily a heaven sent determination infused Caroline as she dangled in the sparse Ladakh air. While I was rambling, her eyes spotted several fissures and cracks crisscrossing the rock face she was suspended against. She willed her legs to grope beneath her and she found secure anchors in the stony crevices. Her fingers and palms gripped rock at the cliff edge. With me still holding on to her wrists, she pulled herself up a few inches.

I heard her breathing. She was gasping and panting far louder than I. Soon her face was level with mine and our eyes met. Hers glittered with cold determination. There was a lost look in mine, she told me later. She was probably right, because she had to shout several times before I paid attention to what she was saying. She wanted me to release her wrists, which I did mechanically. Now, sure of herself, Caroline dragged herself up and without any further incident she flopped beside me. With Tsering looking down on us we lay inert on the rock for several minutes.

After a long time we continued our walk to the crest. The rest of the morning was a blur. None of us were in any state to look for bharal or search for leopards. Kathy, Tina and Yuan turned up, exhausted, after an hour. They had found further sign of the leopard they were following, but had not been able to locate it. We turned back shortly thereafter. Caroline had extracted a promise from Tsering and me not to speak about the morning's drama to anybody. She smiled gratefully when it became clear that we were not going to mention a word. Caroline, in fact, turned distinctly friendly when we maintained our silence at the camp too.

Aditya was aghast when he learned that I had not pursued the leopard with the others. "How could you let such an opportunity go?" he wanted to know. "You were so close to the leopard!" Aditya dismissed the scary wall that had stood between us and the leopard's trail. "Come on, Vikram, if Kathy and Yuan could climb it, so could you. I wish I had been in your group."

Aditya's group had found plenty of leopard scat but no fresh droppings.

"On second thoughts I should be glad that you did not go with them," contended Aditya. "You are going to lose our bet, my friend. There is no way you will spot a snow leopard with your attitude."

Though I protested feebly that the wall was tough, I knew in my heart that I should have climbed it. Aditya was right. My attitude was all wrong. Snow leopards inhabit some of the toughest terrain in the world and I would have to overcome my fear if I was to have any chance of seeing the animal.

In the evening, before dinner, Aditya and Roger play chess while I write my diary. Yuan Lee reads a book. Tsering, poor fellow, is surrounded by Kathy, Tina, Julia and Caroline. The ladies have all decided to teach him English. Raghu and Richard sit outside the dining tent discussing wildlife.

The pout on Caroline's face has vanished. She laughs with the rest of us and there are even flashes of good humour now. I see a look of hope in her mother's eyes. Everyone at the camp is pleasantly surprised with the change in her behaviour.

When night falls, it completely engulfs us. An icy chill clamps down on us and the mountains turn dark and forbidding. There is no light except that of the moon.

Raghu's little radio is our only means of contact with the outside world. He brings it out after dinner and we listen to the news. Wars, revolutions and coups are taking place around the planet. Some politicians are busy making promises, others are sunk deep in scandal. Sitting here in the darkness under the stars, the rest of the world seems so far away. Aditya and I are only interested in the cricket scores. A test match has begun between India and Pakistan. We are both pleased that India has batted well on the first day.

The light of the moon is strong enough for me to see what I write and I bring my diary upto date. It has been a long tiring day. I will troop back to my tent once I am done and I am sure that I will fall asleep as soon as my head touches the pillow.

Day 3

I must say that Raghu's camp is wonderfully organised. I have never had it so good on any camping trip. We are woken every morning at six with the unzipping of our tent flaps. Tashi, the camp boy, greets us with a smile and slips in two mugs of steaming mint tea. A few minutes later Tsewang, Tashi's brother, brings pails of hot water for washing and freshening ourselves. For camp life this is luxury. Additionally, all camp chores like collecting water, cooking and washing are taken care of by the staff. The food here is wonderful and is served in great style in the dining tent.

The daily schedule that was mailed to all the expedition participants reads as:

Typical day:
0600 : Wake and freshen up
0700 : Breakfast
0800 : Begin observations or other field work
1200 : Lunch (often packed, and eaten in the field)
1300 : Continue field work
1700 : Relax and clean up at camp
1900 : Dinner
1930 : Free time

Tina and Raghu ensure that this schedule is followed. Nobody has complained as yet and I don't think anyone will. We are tramping across some of the most breathtaking mountains in the world. Life really couldn't be much better.

Kathy and Richard think so too. According to them this is outdoor life at its best. Our work is tough, challenging and sometimes dangerous, but nobody objects. We toil hard and travel long distances, yet we poke fun at each other and have a good laugh whenever we can. A warm camaraderie is forming between us.

Today, high on a desolate, windy slope we find carvings on a boulder. According to Tina there are several carvings on the mountainsides here. No one knows how old they are. On this particular rock we find hewn out images of blue sheep and humans with bows and arrows. They are simple, childlike drawings, done with the only implements available then – chisel and rock.

This day turns out to be another long one. Like yesterday, our task is to search for leopard sign and the animal's prey. Again we find plenty of evidence of the leopard but no one is lucky enough to lay eyes on the animal. Carrying packed lunches we scoured the mountains in the bright daytime sun and returned only in the evening.

Our inability to spot a snow leopard puzzles me. I can understand the problems of spotting a tiger. Our Indian jungles are heavily forested and a tiger can easily make itself invisible in the thick underbrush. But the mountains here are barren. There is no cover at all and the thin air of Ladakh enables us to see for miles on end. The sharp, crystal-clear visibility is astonishing. We can pick out blue sheep in distant valleys, but why is it so difficult to spot a snow leopard?

In the dining tent, just after dinner, I asked Raghu, why?

"The leopard," he said, leaning back in his chair, "is a master in the art of camouflage. In winter its fur is light coloured and clean, and its body becomes indistinguishable from the snow. In summer its coat collects dust from its surroundings and the leopard takes on a shade similar to the colours of the mountain. But it is not colour alone that hides the animal. The leopard has the uncanny ability to melt into the mountains. It sits so still that it is not possible to see it unless it moves."

There was a time when Raghu had placed a radio-collar on the neck of a snow leopard. The tiny radio transmitter in the collar continuously emitted a signal which Raghu tracked with his receiver. There were many occasions when his receiver pinpointed the animal's location on a mountain opposite him. Raghu would search the mountain slopes till his eyes ached. It was incredibly frustrating. The snow leopard was sitting right in front of Raghu, yet he could not spot it.

Over cups of coffee Raghu told us about the time he had followed snow leopard tracks in the snow. On a winter morning, high on a mountain above Rumbak village, he had come upon fresh tracks. He saw a single set of pug-marks leading across the mountainside. Since the tracks were fresh Raghu had followed them, hoping to find the animal. This was one of the occasions when his luck held. But he did not find a solitary snow leopard as he had thought he would. Instead he found three, a mother and her cubs. They stood silently in the snow, three of the most exquisite animals he had ever seen in his life. It is the occasional heavenly encounter like this which persuades him to keep going, Raghu said. On that day the snow on the slopes was fresh, pure and undisturbed. The air was sharp and nippy. He was alone in the wilderness, just him and the beautiful leopards. We all heard the emotion in Raghu's voice. He obviously had been deeply moved by the encounter. It was one of the most beautiful moments in his life, he recalled.

But Raghu was puzzled because there was only one set of tracks. The only explanation he could muster was that the cubs had followed in the tracks of their mother. It was an astonishing revelation to him. He concluded that stealth and secrecy came naturally to these animals and even at this young stage the cubs had felt a need to mask their presence.

Only once in his life had Raghu been lucky enough to witness the drama of a snow leopard hunt. He had followed the entire episode through his telescope. It happened one evening when he had been watching a herd of argali sheep, the largest of all wild sheep, feeding on the slope of a mountain across the river from where he sat. He almost knocked the telescope over in his excitement when he spotted the leopard. The animal had been within his field of vision for a long time, but he only spotted it when it moved. The leopard was so indiscernible that Raghu almost lost it against the mountainside. Raghu sweated as he watched the animal, praying that he wouldn't lose it. With infinite caution and stealth it closed in on the unsuspecting sheep. The slope was a typical rubble-covered mountainside and the sheep were below and the leopard above. The leopard sometimes dislodged loose stones as he stepped forward. But every time a stone rolled the leopard's paw would dart forward and halt it. The animal would then press the stone back into the ground. Raghu said that it is virtually impossible to move soundlessly on such terrain, yet the snow leopard somehow did. The herd was taken completely by surprise and the leopard managed a kill.

Caroline for some reason was disconcerted with what she had heard. "Does all this mean...are you trying to say that wc will not see a snow leopard?" she enquired.

"Are you lucky at love?" Raghu asked her in reply.

Caroline's blushed. "What kind of a question is that?" she demanded crossly.

"There was a time not long ago, when I was unlucky at love and I saw several snow leopards then. But soon after I got lucky at love and I became distinctly unlucky with snow leopards. I did not see any for a long time."

"I think we had better quit and go home then," said Kathy turning to her husband. "Richard dear, you and I should leave. We have no chance of seeing a leopard since we are deeply in love."

Everyone laughed.

But Caroline was keen to know whether she would see a snow leopard on this trip and she questioned Raghu again.

"There is no clear-cut answer to your question," he told her. "Your group almost found a leopard yesterday. It was somewhere on the mountain you had climbed. Maybe it was sitting right next to you and you passed by the animal without seeing it. You have come to the right place, since these mountains are their home. They are here but it is not easy to spot them."

Raghu adjusted his green hat. "Every animal has to eat, right?" He paused. "The snow leopard is a carnivore. To feed itself it has to follow its prey. In the summer, the snow melts and green pastures open up high in the mountains. Blue sheep, argali, urial, the animals that are the natural prey of the snow leopard move up to these pastures and the leopard follows them. Our next camp is at a higher altitude and we will be visiting the high mountain pastures. That is the best I can do for you; place you where the leopard is most likely to be. Once you are there, sightings depend upon your luck."

"And your love life," chipped in Aditya.

Caroline is a different person now. The dangle in outer space from the cliff edge seems to have transformed her. Her sulky expression has gone and now she is an active member of our team. She has not forgotten the fact that it was Tsering and I who had saved her. Aditya and Roger are jealous of the obvious soft corner she has for the two of us.

But something is wrong between Caroline and her mother. There is an awkwardness between them and they behave like acquaintances rather than friends. I can see that Julia wants to fuss over her daughter and provide her everything she wants. But for some reason Caroline backs away, maintaining a stubborn, unnatural distance from her mother.

Later, the news junkies Raghu, Kathy and Richard listened to the radio. There is so much peace and quiet around us that I wonder why they want to listen to the problems and injustices that plague our planet. The sports news is not very encouraging. India are all out and Pakistan have piled up a huge score without losing any wickets.

Some of us lingered outside the dining tent to watch the stars. I sat with Aditya and Yuan, a woolen cap pulled over my ears and my gloved hands deep in my pockets. Yuan is an expert on stars and he pointed out the galaxies, nebulae, planets and constellations. The cold soon got the better of me and I retired to the warmth of my sleeping bag. It had been another long, tiring and enjoyable day. Once again, like magic, my eyes closed as soon as my head hit my pillow.

Day 4

Aditya and I have not revealed Tsering's true identity to anybody except Raghu. Both of us are bound by an oath of secrecy about the little lama. But in Raghu's case we really had no choice. Aditya had incurred Raghu's wrath by bringing Tsering along uninvited on this trip. As expedition leader Raghu had every right to question Tsering's presence and so we told him the truth. I vividly remember how Raghu's face underwent rapid changes in expression as we related Tsering's story. From barely concealed irritation, his features reflected interest, astonishment and finally wonder. From that moment on he treated Tsering with utmost respect and concern.

Our fellow expedition members were baffled by Raghu's sudden change in attitude to Tsering. After watching the effect of our story on Raghu, I can imagine the astonishment that would have sprung to their faces if I had disclosed that Tsering was a reincarnated lama. They would have been horrified to learn that the little boy had been a prisoner in Tibet for the majority of his nine living years and that he had been freed just a month ago. They would probably have also been incredulous if I had said that during the past two weeks he had been smuggled into India across some of the harshest terrain in the world; then captured twice; and finally liberated by Aditya just a few minutes before our expedition had set off from Leh.* And I am sure that there would have been apprehension amongst them if they had known that Tsering was on the run just now, hiding from an unscrupulous bounty hunter.

* Related in 'Ladakh Adventure'

We are not sure of what to do with young Tsering. Aditya and I are not authorised to take decisions for the boy. We need instructions from his well-wishers in Leh. But unfortunately, up here in the mountains we are cut off from the rest of the world. There is no mobile network, telephone or any other means of communication. Some kind of postal system exists but it is rather inefficient. The postman visits this area only once a month. Raghu had suggested an alternate mail system to us. The horseman Karma was to return to Leh with his pack animals to bring supplies for our camp. I had sent a note with Karma to our guardian, *Meme* Chacko. Karma has returned this morning from Leh with an envelope from him, for Aditya and me.

Dear Vikram and Aditya,

Tsering's safety has been uppermost on the minds of several people these last few days. There was widespread dismay when he disappeared. The people at Dharamshala were extremely upset when they learned of his abduction. But relief quickly replaced their apprehension when they heard about his rescue.*

The people of Dharamshala have requested me to convey their gratitude and sincere appreciation to you both. You have done them a great favour by protecting an extremely important member of their community. I too am deeply relieved that the boy is safe and well. My congratulations to you, Aditya, for masterminding his safe release.

The question now is what do we do with Tsering? Our objective is to deliver him safely to Dharamshala. I wish the task was as simple as arranging transport for the boy. Unfortunately, it is not. Leh is a dangerous place for Tsering. It is swarming with his abductors who have even been asking questions at the lodge where you were staying. I have it from reliable sources that your lodge is under surveillance. Queries have been made at Dolma's

* Dharamshala is the Indian home of all Tibetian Buddhists

restaurant too and her movements are being tracked. I believe that I too am being followed.

I have been in constant touch with the people at Dharamshala and we have been consulting each other on how to proceed in this matter. After a lot of deliberation we have concluded that the safest place for Tsering is with you, in the Rumbak valley. You have disappeared without a trace and your vanishing act has stumped Tsering's abductors.

Dharamshala requests that you keep Tsering with you. Tell Tsering that his people are organising a team to collect him soon. They will come in two bus loads from Dharamshala — they obviously believe in safety in numbers. With so many people to protect the little lama it is unlikely that his abductors will launch another attempt on him. The team will drive up from Dharamshala and then walk on to Rumbak and escort him to Leh from there. You should expect them in a few days.

Other news that might interest you is that your friend the Japanese man has gone underground. There is no trace of him here in Leh. He has disappeared from the hotel which Aditya and Dolma discovered and he no longer visits 'Nirvana Travels'. But he obviously is somewhere here. I have no doubt that he is controlling this very thorough operation to search for Tsering.

I suspect that we are all being trailed. I had to take special precautions when I heard that a horseman from Rumbak had arrived with a message for me. I did not personally meet the horseman to collect your note, and afterwards I arranged for somebody else to hand my reply to him.

I warn you both not to take the threat to Tsering lightly. His pursuers want him at any cost. Do not let him out of your sight. You need to be vigilant only for a few more days, till the team from Dharamshala takes over.

I am leaving for the Changthang plateau today. One more family of blacknecked cranes has been located and I hope I can find them. I shall keep this trip short because of the Tsering problem and return in two or three days. Keep up the good work. I will be in touch with you soon.

Sincerely,
Col. Tommy Chacko

"I don't think Tsering will mind," commented Aditya after reading the letter. "A few extra days with us should be alright with him. He is quite happy here, what with everybody fussing over him."

Aditya was right. Tsering has integrated well with our group. His impish smile has endeared him to everybody. We have also generated a good deal of sympathy for the boy through the story we fabricated about him. There were several questions about him and since we cannot disclose his identity, we used our imagination and contrived a story about him. We have told everybody that Tsering is a Tibetan refugee who has lost his parents. Aditya explained that his father had adopted Tsering during his posting in Ladakh last year and is paying for Tsering's education at a Tibetan school. Since the school is closed for a month we have brought him here with us. We have informed everybody that Tsering would be pleased to learn English during his free time here. The ladies have taken up the challenge and Tsering has a lot of work in the evenings.

Aditya and I teach him Hindi, and Tina, Julia and Kathy teach him English. Tsering, to his credit, has proved himself to be a quick learner and communication at the basic level has begun.

We were able to convey the contents of *Meme* Chacko's letter quite easily to him. His red-cheeked face remained expressionless while he absorbed the news. His eyes are deep luminous pools and it is impossible to read them. He did not say anything for a few minutes. Then with a big grin he told us in his tortured Hindi that he was excited to hear that people from Dharamshala were coming. These were his people and though he had never been there, he was aware that Dharamshala was going to be his Indian home in the years to come.

"What an ungrateful little fellow," complained Aditya. "Look at him. We go through all this trouble rescuing him and all he is excited about is leaving us and going to Dharamshala."

Tsering is a canny little boy and he handled Aditya's friendly tirade with aplomb. He imperiously informed Aditya that he should be grateful for the blessings and company of a holy lama. There was a dazzling twinkle in his eyes as he spoke and all three of us laughed.

We would all miss Tsering. The little lama had worked his way into our hearts. Aditya, despite his tough-guy image has a special relationship with the boy. The ladies in our group treat him like their own child. Everybody, including the camp boys and the cooks, have realised that Tsering is somebody special. The reception party has probably set off from Dharamshala. They could arrive tomorrow, maybe the day after. One or two days; that is all the time we have left with our little lama.

But danger and uncertainty still surround Tsering. *Meme* Chacko, in his letter, has once more warned us about the Japanese man. Though outwitted twice the man refuses to go away. We never had any idea of the Japanese man's identity; this despite him having chased us from Tso Kar to Leh. It was Aditya who finally found out about the man. During his dramatic rescue effort Aditya had sneaked into the Japanese man's hotel room and come across airline tickets drawn in the name of a Mr. Akira. The final confirmation of his identity was unveiled through a report that was handed to Raghu and me just before we left Leh.

My father's dear friend, uncle Reddy, who is the chief forest officer of Ranthambore and also a man I respect and admire, had handed us the report. Raghu and I were to attend a talk that uncle Reddy was especially flying down from Delhi to deliver. Unfortunately, his flight came in late and since we were leaving on that same day at noon, we could not attend the talk. Uncle Reddy however, handed us a copy of a report he had prepared, saying that most of what he planned to talk about was covered in the report. There had been no time to read it then and I, in truth, forgot about it till Raghu handed it to me on the second day of our expedition.

Aditya and I had instantly recognised the photograph attached to the report and the name matched that which Aditya had seen on the airline tickets. The Japanese man who had ruined our Tso Kar trip and spoiled our stay at Leh finally had a name – Mr. Akira Singh. Both Aditya and I read the report over and over again. Its contents confirmed that we were pitted against a formidable opponent. *Meme* Chacko had clearly conveyed in his letter that Akira had not given up his quest for Tsering. We would have to maintain our guard until we handed Tsering over to his friends from Dharamshala.

Today we believe we came close to spotting a snow leopard. The incident took place sometime during the late afternoon. Our team was walking along the slope of a difficult mountain when suddenly a shower of gravel and stones rained down on us.

"Blue sheep!" exclaimed Tina staring upwards.

They were quite distant from us, high up on the mountain, and we had to strain our necks to observe them. It was a small group. There were five grey specks and I recognised them as blue sheep only when I gazed at them through my binoculars. They were gathered on a cliff above us, balanced precariously on its precipitous edge. I am sure that they were aware of our presence below them, yet none of them spared us a glance. Instead they stared watchfully back along the slope they had run down.

"Leopard," Tina said excitedly. "I am sure it is a leopard that has scared the animals."

We eagerly scanned the slope with our binoculars.

"Search the area the sheep are gazing at," Tina instructed us.

The frightened animals were staring at a large field of boulders. With binoculars glued to our eyes, we stood in a line: Kathy, Caroline, Yuan, Tina, Tsering and I. Our necks were tilted backwards at an uncomfortable angle. An expectant thrill must have been running through each of us but it was Caroline who was the most excited. When I glanced at her I saw that her jaw was open and her hands were shaking. There was a breathlessness to her voice. She kept asking Tina where to look. We scanned the slope till our eyes ached. All I saw was boulders and empty scree slopes. The sheep continued to gaze at the boulders, not dropping their guard. After about ten minutes the sheep began to shuffle away. Holding fast to the edge of the cliff they disappeared around a bend in the mountain.

"Blue sheep run to a cliff edge when they are attacked," said Raghu, when we described our experience to him later that evening. "It is the most logical place for them to flee to. Their predators are not as comfortable as they are on precipitous edges. Carnivores think twice about attacking at such dangerous places because the momentum of their attack can carry them over the edge. Falling gravel alerted you when the sheep fled and collected at the brink. I think that a snow leopard must have attacked just then. The leopard was right there, exactly where you and the sheep were staring. But..."

"But we didn't see the animal!" Caroline finished for him.

There was disappointment written all over the American girl's face. We were all disappointed but Caroline was by far the most affected. I couldn't understand why she was so distraught. All right, the leopard had been there in front of our eyes. So what? It was nothing to mope about. In fact the rest of us were thrilled. We felt privileged to have witnessed the animal's talent of melting into the mountainside. Kathy said that she now understood why the leopard was called the 'grey ghost' of the Himalaya.

Caroline, however, did not agree with us. The pout returned to her face and she sulked through the evening. Her quiet and gentle mother tried to console her, only to be rudely turned away. An embarrassing scene took place when Caroline shouted at her mother and stomped away. Poor Julia. She smiled disconcertedly at us and apologised for her daughter's behaviour. This constant rejection of the mother intrigues me and I wonder what the problem is.

The one person who is happy with our failure to spot the animal is Aditya. He remembers our bet and doesn't want to lose it.

There was no let up for Tsering at camp. Kathy and Tina pounced on him in the evening and subjected him to their English tutelage. Caroline sat alone in her tent. I searched and found myself a corner some distance from the camp and wrote my diary. But by hiding myself from the others I missed an outing on which I should have gone. Raghu took the others on an excursion to show them a golden eagle's nest. Everyone was thrilled to see a nesting pair high on a steep rock face. The chick had been hatched, and while one parent stayed beside the nest, the other departed on frequent forays in search of food.

Raghu's radio informed us that there had been heavy shelling at the town of Kargil. The Pakistani forces on the mountains above had rained artillery fire on the town. It is hard to believe that there is a war going on barely a 100 kilometres from here.

"I don't understand this," said Richard sucking at his pipe. "Your two countries are fighting a war and playing a friendly game of cricket at the same time. It doesn't make any sense."

"It is the war over Kashmir," said Raghu. "Pakistan says that Kashmir belongs to them. India says that Kashmir belongs to us. We've been fighting over it for several decades. I admit that it does sound crazy; fighting on the battlefield and on the cricket field at the same time. But it at least provides a bright side to the madness of war. Who knows, maybe the friendship we find on the cricket field might one day be extended to the battle field."

I shivered in the night cold. People were running to bomb shelters just a few hours away from where we were. I wished we had not listened to the news. The peace and calm that enveloped us suddenly evaporated into the thin Ladakh air like an illusion. I felt vulnerable and insecure.

The weather bureau sharpened my anxiety. There were severe snowstorms in the Himalayas. The passes were blocked and emergencies had been declared in certain areas. Here, just a short distance north of the great Himalayan ridge, we could see the stars. There was not even a hint of the terrible weather to the south.

Not all the news is disheartening. India is doing well in the test match. Pakistan have been bowled out cheaply after a promising start. Aditya and I think India is better placed than Pakistan. But Richard and Roger think otherwise and back Pakistan. We strike a ten rupee wager.

Bidding good night to one another, most of us dispersed after the news. Tina and Raghu remained behind along with Richard. The data we collected over the last two days has to be catalogued and put away. Our work in this area is completed and we are moving on to the high mountain pastures tomorrow.

I returned to my tent along with Tsering. I must have been in a disturbed state of mind because my eyes did not close as they usually did when my head hit the pillow.

Day 5

We broke camp early in the morning and followed the winding Rumbak river. Climbing steadily we soon spotted snow-capped peaks ahead of us. The sun was out and we sweated from our exertion. We reached the Rumbak valley before noon.

The narrow gorge suddenly widened and we found ourselves on a large plateau. We saw a big tent pitched to the left of our path. There were many ponies grazing beside the tent and as we approached we saw weary tourists sitting outside clutching steaming mugs. The tent is a refreshment stop, the only one in this area. It is a place where trekkers can pause, gather their breath and swallow some nourishment. We stopped here and ordered mint tea and biscuits.

Rumbak is a tiny village with very few households. There are fields here and it is refreshing to see the colour green again. The village is nestled in a curving valley through which a glacial stream runs. The houses are typical flat-roofed Ladakhi houses and are widely spaced amongst the fields. There are Buddhist flags everywhere and I spot big pyramid-like chortens. It is a lonely village, quiet and beautiful in the noonday sun.

Our camp boys Tashi and Tsewang, and the horseman, Karma, are from Rumbak. We extend our halt so that they can meet their friends and relatives. After a long rest we move on. The river valley is extremely wide now. The walls of the mountains are smooth, unlike the tortured, broken mountainsides we travelled through earlier. These, according to Raghu, have been smoothened by glaciers which had once occupied this valley. With the emergence of warmer weather they had retreated and were now restricted to the peaks of only the highest mountains.

We climbed steadily up the wide valley till we were confronted by a broad, steep mountain. Here the valley branched into two arms and this was where our expedition split up. Tina was to lead her group into the valley on the left and Raghu would lead his group along the right branch. The ponies, luggage, camp boys and cooks were to be divided between the two teams. The teams were to meet up again in three days. The idea was to cover two different valleys at the same time, thereby widening the scope of the research.

Aditya was not happy to bid goodbye to Tsering. "Look after him," he told me. "We don't want him disappearing again."

Caroline's mother hugged her. Richard kissed Kathy goodbye.

There has been no change in the composition of the teams that had been formed on the first day. Our group which set off along the left bank of the valley consisted of Tina, Kathy, Caroline, Yuan Lee, Tsering and myself. Wangchuk, the cook, and Tashi, the camp boy, accompanied us. After a long uphill walk, we rounded a bend and were confronted with a stunning view of glacier-capped mountains. So near did they seem that I felt I could reach out and touch them.

We reached our campsite late in the afternoon, after a two-hour uphill slog. This was the camp below the glaciers that Raghu had told us about. From here the peaks are continuous snow-pyramids above us. The massive walls of ice are clearly visible now. A cliff of ice cloaks the mountain Stok Kangri. The ice is blue on top and dark and muddy at the bottom. Too bad Aditya isn't here; this is the campsite for which he had longed. Both Tsering and I miss him but it is comforting to know that he will be with us in a few days.

Our campsite has a flattened section outside our tents and in the evening I stand there marvelling at the view. There are mountains wherever I look. It is a humbling sight – one that I have never seen before. It is not that I am new to mountains. My school is in the Nilgiris and I see them every day. But the Ladakh mountains are very different from my Nilgiri ones. There are no trees here to soften their edges and their slopes are bare and naked. There must be hundreds of mountains surrounding me. Stark, rocky pyramids pile up one after the other, like the waves of an endless sea. The colour green is absent and I see only shades of brown and purple. This is a mountain wilderness and it overwhelms me. I understand how lonely and insignificant I am as I watch the sun disappear behind a distant, jagged line of peaks.

Tonight, for the second night, I did not fall asleep easily. In fact, I lay awake for quite a while. I wondered whether it was the altitude as I tossed and turned. This campsite is more than 16,000 feet above sea level. But my breathing was normal and I wasn't suffering from a headache. Maybe it was the absence of Aditya. I always feel comforted by his presence. I was nervous. Looking after Tsering is a huge responsibility. Aditya and I had shared the responsibility till today. Now I am alone.

Day 6

Radio contact has been established with Raghu's camp. We speak to them at prearranged timings: at eight, before we set off on our day's work and at eight, after dinner. This morning it was Tina who spoke first to Raghu, discussing and finalising plans for the day. Then, I spoke to Aditya.

He was in good spirits. His camp was not beneath the glaciers and he was jealous of us. He wanted to talk to Tsering but before he did he asked me to speak to somebody – it was a surprise, he said.

And what a surprise it was!

I found myself speaking to our Swedish friends, Anders and his wife Eva. We had met the couple a week earlier, at the eastern edge of Ladakh. But what were they doing in the Rumbak area? They were supposed to be on a bicycle trip.

Anders, in his accented English, explained that their bicycle ride had been cut short when the front wheel of his bike had been smashed beyond repair. While they had parked at the roadside for lunch – imagine, 'parked' he repeated – a truck had backed into his bicycle. Yes, it was a terribly disappointing end to their trip, but instead of crying about the mishap they had decided to take it in their stride. The aborted trip had resulted in a few extra days in Ladakh with nothing to do. A travel agent had suggested that they undertake a short trek in the Hemis National Park. They knew that we were out here somewhere and they had found Aditya's camp.

"What are your plans?" I asked.

Anders said that Raghu had no objection to their spending a few days with the expedition, as long as they contributed to the team effort. Both he and Eva were excited at the prospect of working in our group and were looking forward to meeting Tsering and me.

I had to release the radio soon since Tina was getting impatient. Tsering hurriedly spoke to Aditya and the Swedes and then we set off.

For once our work has nothing to do with blue sheep or snow leopards. Our task today is to survey the vegetation on the mountains. Now that we are at a higher altitude, the mountains are distinctly greener. Raghu and Tina already have satellite photographs of this area. We have to compare the vegetation on the ground with that of their photographs. Tina is a hard taskmaster and we spent the entire day walking along slopes noting the type of vegetation we came across.

The weather has deteriorated today. The snowstorms from the south have finally had an effect here. It is cloudy and at this altitude we distinctly feel the cold. The glaciers are hidden behind curtains of swirling mist. We long for the sun but it spends the day behind dense cloud.

The inclement weather influences the mood at camp and our talk is subdued. My fingers are frozen and I find it difficult to write. The women lack the spirit for an English lesson and Tsering is happy to have a rest day. There is a fiery sunset in the evening and we all regretfully watch the sun go down.

As darkness sweeps across the heavens, the weather begins to lift. We see the moon and stars appear one by one in the spaces between the clouds. At eight I speak to Aditya on the radio. He informs me that rain has washed out play in the test match. I asked about the weather forecast. It seems that storms have wreaked havoc in the Himalayas. All vehicular traffic to Leh has come to a halt because the passes are snowbound. The good news, according to the weather bureau, is that the disturbance is expected to ease tomorrow. Hopefully the sun will return.

The clouds are dispersing and stars crowd the skies. The passes are blocked. I wonder whether Tsering's people from Dharamshala have made it through. They are scheduled to show up at Rumbak tomorrow. I secretly hope that they are stuck.

It is cold at this altitude. I pull on two sweaters and crawl into my sleeping bag. Soon my shivering ceases and I begin to feel warm and quickly fall asleep.

[illegible] that the discipline [illegible]
[illegible]

[illegible] and [illegible] The
[illegible]
[illegible]
[illegible] that they are
[illegible]

[illegible] and travel
[illegible]
[illegible]

The Final Hours

The Magical Meadow

All traces of the storm that had struck the Himalayas had disappeared. The sky had been washed clean and sparkled a crystal blue overhead. Every peak that soared above the campsite was bathed in sunlight, but lower down the valleys were filled with shadows. Vikram gaped in awe at the scale of the shadows. They were gigantic, some stretching several kilometres. The shadows blanketing the campsite, however, had been banished earlier as the sun cleared the peaks to the east. Tsering, Tina, Kathy, Yuan and Vikram stood in a line enjoying the warmth of its golden rays.

Having suffered bitterly cold weather the previous day, they now revelled in the sun's warmth. Tsering had discarded his sweater and was attired in only a T-shirt and jeans. Tina, Kathy and Yuan had also peeled off their warm outer layers. The brilliant blue sky promised a warm, sunny day but Vikram, who was cautious by nature, did not remove his protective clothing. He stood beside his friends bundled beneath a thick sweater and jacket. The group was waiting for Caroline who was always the last to report in the morning.

Tashi, the camp boy, came around handing out lunch boxes. Tashi as usual had a cheerful grin on his face. "Good food today, sir," he told Vikram as he handed him a steel box.

"That's what you tell us everyday," said Yuan accepting his box. Yuan was fed up of *parathas* and eggs. He sorely missed his traditional Chinese meals.

"Ladakh food always good, sir," beamed the young boy.

"Not like Chinese food," he said cheekily.

"What's wrong with Chinese food?" enquired Yuan.

"Spicy... HOT!" Tashi hopped energetically and shook his jaw, imitating a mouth on fire. In the process a lunch box slipped from his hand and cracked open on the ground, spilling its contents. Tashi clasped his mouth in consternation and shot a guilty glance at Tina. The frosty stare that came his way thoroughly chastened the boy. He scooped up the wasted meal and hastily returned to the kitchen tent. Caroline appeared shortly, grinning apologetically, and after Tashi delivered a fresh lunch box they set off.

The instructions Raghu had radioed earlier were to search above the camp for blue sheep. The slopes above Tina's camp were visible from Raghu's campsite. Late the previous evening, Raghu had noticed movement on those mountains. Though the light wasn't good and the mountaintops were swathed in mist, Raghu was convinced that he had spotted a herd of bharal.

The top of the mountain was what Raghu had said and so they trudged upwards. Vikram quickly discarded his jacket, rolling it and stuffing it into his backpack. His sweater followed shortly. Sweat poured from all of them and their breath came in deep gulps. They halted frequently, gasping and clutching their hips. It was a long, tiresome journey. They often looked upwards, searching for the end of their climb, but the mountain seemed to go on and on and on. After what seemed like an eternity they topped a steep incline and emerged on a level section of land.

"Oh no!" groaned Caroline as she slumped to the ground. "We're not even halfway there."

A massive hump of rock ahead was the reason for her dismay. The mountain had only taken a pause. An extensive plateau-like surface lay before them and at its distant end the upward slope continued.

"Bharal!" exclaimed Tina, reaching for her binoculars,

but the rest of the group paid no heed to her excited call. Their enthusiasm for blue sheep was dampened by their exhaustion and instead of grabbing their binoculars they flopped to the ground.

"You won't need to climb to the top of the mountain," assured Tina as she gazed through her lenses. "The sheep have descended to the plateau we are standing on. I can see a small group of them." There was a short silence before she continued. "They have disappeared around a bend. Something tells me that there is a good grazing site there. Cheer up you lazy lot, I think we have found Raghu's herd."

After a refreshing drink from their water-bottles and a long rest they set off once more. The level ground they walked across was huge. There was enough space here for fifty cricket grounds, thought Vikram. "Wow!" he breathed as they trudged forward. He was now beginning to understand the immenseness of the Himalaya.

The ground underfoot began to change. A sprinkling of grass had appeared. There were tiny green clumps widely spaced amidst the rubble and rock. Soon the clumps began to bunch together and Vikram spied tiny yellow flowers. Desert was yielding to mountain meadow. Marmot burrows appeared and Vikram spotted the furry creatures staring warily at them from the safety of their holes.

They found the sheep after an hour's hard walking. Tina's mouth popped open when she saw the size of the herd. The valley ahead was crawling with bharal; there were well over a hundred of them. With great excitement, telescopes, cameras and binoculars were plucked from backpacks. Tina settled her group at an acceptable distance from the herd. She instructed them to speak only in whispers and not to make any sudden movements that might disturb the animals.

"This is one of the largest herds I have ever seen," she breathed. Her eyes sparked with suppressed excitement. "If they allow us, we will stay with them through the day, and note down observations. Raghu has already taught you how to record their movements. The data that you compile today will be published in wildlife journals. So please concentrate and be as accurate as possible."

Everybody worked diligently. The animals were congregated in two separate groups. Caroline, Vikram and Kathy gathered data on one of the groups while Tina, Tsering and Yuan worked on the other. Their task was to maintain an activity chart of the herd. They had to continuously observe and count the number of animals sitting, standing, grazing, sleeping, playing or standing sentry. They were to take notes of where the animals preferred to locate themselves and how close they stood to escape avenues like cliffs and rock faces. Their actions had to be recorded every five minutes.

Before this encounter Vikram had only seen blue sheep foraging on distant mountaintops. Now the animals were barely 300 metres away and he was gazing at them down the barrel of a telescope. The goat-like creatures were about the same size as Ladakhi ponies and their predominant colour was a greyish-brown which merged well with their surroundings. Their bellies were white and their tails small and black. Females had thin, small horns while the males had large, curving ones.

Vikram found himself enjoying his work. There was constant activity within the herd. Young bharal chased their playmates. Adult males brandished their headgear, playfully butting each other. There was no rough fighting. The primary objective of the herd was to feed and they spent most of their time doing just that.

The sun was warm on their backs and the high mountain air was crisp. Lunch was consumed while they worked. Between observations Vikram found time to look around him. Marmots were everywhere on the slopes. He and Caroline had a contest looking for the fattest one. The furry creatures seemed incredibly lazy. They spent most of their time sitting by their burrows staring into space. The marmots were enjoying the afternoon, basking in the sun and taking in the cloudless blue sky. Two months of summer still remained – two months to play, feed and make merry. Then, like all good things, summer would come to an end and they would be faced with the daunting prospect of a season of bitter cold and no food. The onset of winter would signal the time for hibernation. It was the fat built up by their ceaseless feeding which would enable them to survive their long sleep through the winter. Life would come full circle for the marmots in spring when they would wake once again, ravenously hungry and ready for a season of food and play.

It was the promise of finding a herd of bharal that had lured Vikram and his companions up the unending slopes of this mountain. Their toil and sweat had been well rewarded he thought as he gazed around him. Till now mountains had always soared above them. Now for the first time Vikram was actually looking down on their peaks and from here he had an aerial view of the rugged territory through which they had passed. The Rumbak valley was visible below. Vikram remembered the enormous amounts of energy he had expended to get to the valley and its village; now he was high above them.

Vikram felt good to be up here. What thrilled him more than anything else was the accomplishment of having reached the snowline. Their uphill march had brought them level with the snowline and the glaciers. A huge pyramid of ice and snow stretched behind the herd. The glacier that capped the mountain ahead was streaked with distinct horizontal lines. Its upper section reflected the colour of the sky and was a bright, transparent blue. The lowest section, the part that is called the tongue, was muddy and streaked with dirt. Vikram and his camp mates had climbed so high that the tongue of the glacier was actually below them.

During the early afternoon Tina showed them how to

tell the difference between young and adult sheep and to gauge the age of the animals. Together they worked out the composition of the herd, dividing it into male, female and various age groups. The count was 224 animals – the largest herd Tina had ever seen.

Time slipped by. The herd had found an excellent pasture and they were content to spend the day feeding and resting. Sometime during the latter part of the afternoon the wind picked up. It was a mild breeze to start with but it soon turned into a minor gale. It whistled steadily past the group, stinging their cheeks and numbing their fingers. They were seated on the exposed side of the mountain and there was no escape for them. Vikram slipped on his sweater and then his jacket and gloves. Caroline was the only other member of the group carrying warm clothing. The rest were dressed in T-shirts and light sweaters and they soon began to freeze. The wind numbed them, scornfully piercing their clothing. The blazing sun did little to relieve the cold. Though Tsering's cheeks remained red, those of Kathy, Tina and Yuan turned blue. Their hands began to lose feeling and simple actions like holding binoculars or scribbling notes turned painful and labourious. The change in the weather did not perturb the sheep. Unaffected, they continued to feed. The wind blew silently without letting up and it rapidly became evident that they would have to leave. Tina was deeply disappointed. She was being forced to cut short a wonderful opportunity to gather data.

Vikram and Caroline volunteered to stay behind and continue observations till dark. Tina was thankful for their offer but was reluctant to split the group so high on the mountain. Their safety was her responsibility. It was not an easy decision for Tina but eventually it was her thirst for wildlife data that prevailed.

So long as they behaved in a responsible manner they could stay behind. By 'responsible' she meant that they should quit at least an hour before sunset. "I don't want you two stuck on the slopes in the dark," she warned. "You won't be able to judge where to place your feet and one wrong step can result in serious injuries."

Tsering grinned sheepishly at Vikram before leaving. "Sorry..." he began in Hindi, but Caroline cut him off insisting that he speak in English. With Caroline's help, and more in Hindi than English, Tsering conveyed that he was sorry to leave them. It was his fault, he should have brought his warm clothes along.

"You lucky darlings," whispered Kathy kissing them both on their cheeks. "I wish I could have stayed with you. Maybe I should learn from you, Vikram, and always be prepared for the worst."

"Maybe you should," grinned Vikram.

Caroline and Vikram waved good-bye to their friends and got back to work. Caroline used the telescope while Vikram peered at the sheep through binoculars.

"This is fun," remarked Caroline after their next set of observations.

"It is," agreed Vikram, jotting his readings.

After scrawling another set of readings Caroline spoke again. "Never in my wildest dreams did I ever think that I would enjoy this trip, Vikram." She shook her head. "Today I believe camp life is fun. But before I came here I had dreaded the very thought of it, thinking that it would be a horrible, smelly, unhygienic existence. Even the mountains – these awesome, majestic mountains – I can't imagine that at one time I was terrified of them. I was mortally scared of this trip, so scared that I made myself sick. I really did not want to come."

"Then why did you?" asked Vikram.

Caroline did not reply immediately. Her throat quivered. There was turmoil within her and Vikram could sense it. It was evident that she wanted to speak; she needed to unburden herself. Caroline's story unfolded slowly, in fits and starts.

"It was I who decided to come here. Mom was taken aback when I asked her to buy tickets to Ladakh, India. She asked me whether I was sure. She wanted to know whether I knew what I was getting myself into. She talked to me, she tried to caution me but I refused to listen and insisted that she buy the tickets. Mom, of course, was right. In my typical thoughtless manner, I was stepping blindly into this trip. It was only as the day of our departure neared that the enormity of what I had taken on began to sink in. I was going to be leaving the United States for the first time in my life; leaving it for a country I knew precious little about. Yes, my grandfather was from here, but he passed away before I was born. My mother, though she is half-Indian, has rarely spoken to me about this country. Even at school they don't teach us much about India. All I knew was that there are many people here and that there are temples, cows and tigers. They did teach us about the mighty Himalaya, the greatest mountain range in the world. But I did not know that the Himalaya were here, in India."

Caroline broke off as they concentrated on observing the animals. She continued after the next sets of readings were recorded.

"I did not want to leave home and the United States, but I couldn't back out because I would lose face with mom. I hated every moment of this trip; from the flight into Delhi and then onto Leh. There were those terrible days we spent acclimatising in Leh, when I could hardly breathe. I was really miserable then; there was nothing to look forward to except an exhausting climb high into the mountains where there was even less oxygen and the horrible prospect of camp life. The lowest point of this journey was my falling into that hole."

Caroline laughed. Her eyes twinkled and sunlight flashed on her teeth. "My spirits sank really low that morning. Things could not have got any worse. There had to be a turning point and it was you who set me right. The turning came during those moments I spent, as you say, suspended in space, dangling from your hands. I have never undergone such radical treatment. It shook me thoroughly. I needed something like that Vikram; that single incident straightened me out."

Vikram remained silent, allowing Caroline to speak.

"For the first time I was honest with myself. After taking a hard look at my behaviour and at myself I finally realised the obvious. My problem was me. It was something that was clearly evident to all of you. Everyone knew that it was I – I who was making myself miserable. That dangle in outer space knocked the blinkers off my eyes and I saw the truth. I saw that I was surrounded by wonderful, caring people. I discovered that our daily escapades were actually great fun. This expedition is a fantastic outdoor experience. I can't believe that I was unhappy when I should have felt privileged to be here in these mountains. Everything has changed since those horrible days, Vikram. Even just sitting up here beside this magical meadow, watching these sheep, is fun!"

"Your behaviour..." Vikram shook his head, "...the less said about it, the better. For a moment while you dangled there I seriously considered letting you go. The world might have been a better place if...ouch!"

Caroline smacked Vikram's head.

"Hey...I was only joking," he protested as Caroline raised her hand once more. The girl halted, smiling, and they both laughed.

They continued their work companionably. The wind eased around four thirty, subsiding to a breeze, and then stopped altogether. At five the herd began to move. A few males gathered and started walking slowly, and soon the rest began to follow. Caroline and Vikram trailed behind. The animals led them along a stony, wide shelf, directly towards the glaciers.

The herd ambled along, in no hurry at all. The ledge

widened into a huge sloping plain before terminating at the foot of a massive wall of ice. The snow-covered peak of the mountain seemed so close that Vikram felt he could get there in under an hour. That was, of course, if he could cross the hulking glacier that lay between him and the top. The glacier was golden in the evening sun. Despite its serene beauty Vikram knew better than to even dream of attempting it.

Melt-water flowed from hundreds of tiny rivulets beneath the ice. They had reached the source of the Rumbak river. It was quite an achievement thought Vikram. They had travelled the river's entire length; from its confluence with the Indus, to its birthplace in the mountains. The water was a pure, sparkling blue and they could hear its muted roar amidst the mountain silence.

Shadows were lengthening and the evening chill was making its presence felt. The herd was walking to the far end of the ledge. There was a way out from the glacier bound valley; Vikram could see a pass to the right of the glacier where, perhaps, the herd was headed.

But time had run out for Caroline and Vikram and they turned regretfully away from the sheep. As they trudged slowly back towards the grassy meadow Vikram pointed to a neighbouring slope on which animals appeared to be grazing.

"Yaks," said Caroline, staring through her binoculars. "Yaks and dzos."

How small they looked, mused Vikram. The huge animals were so far away that they were reduced to tiny dots, strung along an immense mountainside. Vikram stared at the animals, marvelling at the clarity with which he could see them. There was no haze or dust to obscure his vision.

Up here at 17,000 feet there were green grasslands, but down at the base of the mountains it was barren and desert-like. What startling contrasts thought Vikram. Ladakh was a land that thrilled him. It ignited a deep sense of wonder within him and he knew for certain that it had found a permanent place in his heart.

Bad News

They returned to the spot where they had spent the day and packed their telescopes, binoculars, notepads and lunch boxes. Then shouldering their packs they set off on their long journey back to camp.

The mountaintops turned golden and shadows smothered the valleys. Vikram heard a loud, whistle-like sound. Looking in the direction of the sound he spotted several creatures scrambling up the hill. They were grey-brown birds. Snowcocks! Yes, the birds were a family of snowcocks waddling away from them. Below, in the shadowy valleys, Vikram spied a circling flock of yellow-billed choughs. The birds were like large black crows, except that they had yellow bills. They were flying high above the valley floor, yet they were way below him.

"Somebody's coming," said Caroline. She was gazing westwards, shielding her eyes with her hand. A speck had appeared at the far edge of the plateau.

Caroline raised her binoculars. "I think it's Tashi."

It was Tashi alright. His was a lonely figure on the yellow, sun-kissed mountainside. Vikram frowned. Why was the boy running? "Something's wrong," he told Caroline. "He is sprinting hard. Let's hurry."

The two teenagers ran.

The plateau was immense, fifty cricket pitches, recollected Vikram. Shadows engulfed the mountains and by the time Vikram and Caroline reached Tashi's side only the glaciers remained free from their conquering darkness. The Ladakhi boy's cheeks were flushed. Fear knotted Vikram's stomach when he saw the expression on Tashi's face.

Tashi wheezed and gasped. He spoke in Hindi. "Men... many men," he breathed. "They attacked the camp after Tina madam returned. I saw...I was washing dishes at the river. They have guns. Everybody is prisoner."

"Tsering!" cried Vikram. "Where is Tsering?"

"I saw them take Tsering away. I was watching from behind some rocks. Three men walked with him towards Rumbak. Tina madam and the rest of the *saabs* and *memsaabs* have been left behind at the camp. They are being guarded."

Vikram stared at Tashi in horror. Tsering had been abducted. Akira had struck.

"What's the matter?" enquired Caroline worriedly.

Vikram did not reply. His shoulders sagged.

"I was behind the river boulders," continued Tashi, regaining his breath. "There were seven men. They tied everybody's hands and feet and made them sit in a line and then took Tsering away. They tied him to a pony and led the animal back towards Rumbak. Before they left, their leader had a long talk with Tina madam. Maybe they wanted to know where you had gone. Tina madam must have given them wrong directions because after some time two men started climbing. They did not climb this slope, but instead they headed towards the glacier, from the far side. I stole away, creeping through the boulders, till a mountain shielded me from the camp. Then I started climbing."

"Vikram!" Caroline was angry. "Will you tell me what's going on?"

Vikram translated Tashi's story.

The girl's mouth popped open. She stared in disbelief. "What...are you out of your mind? Men, guns, everybody captured? What are you talking about?"

But Vikram was not looking at her. There was movement on the mountainside. Blue sheep were streaming onto the plateau. It was the same group they had followed to the glacier-bound valley.

"Not now, Caroline." There was a ring of urgency in his voice. "Something has disturbed the bharal. Look, they have turned around and they're coming back out of the valley we had followed them into. Tashi, were those men headed towards the glacier above the sheep? Is it the men who are disturbing the sheep?"

"Yes, Vikram *saab*," replied the boy. "It could be them; there is a pass into that ice valley and the men were climbing towards that pass."

Vikram thought quickly. The camp was being guarded. Attempting to rescue his friends would not be a wise idea. But it wasn't his friends he was worried about, it was Tsering — only Tsering mattered.

Caroline watched in bewilderment as Vikram and Tashi talked in Hindi.

"Are you sure they have taken Tsering to Rumbak?" questioned Vikram.

"I think so," replied Tashi. "I heard the man who was in charge shout as he walked away with Tsering. He told his men that he was halting at Rumbak. It is too late to walk to Leh now, *saab*. They will have to walk in the dark. It is sensible to halt at the village."

"Tashi, we need a place to hide. Those sheep are moving fast and that worries me." Turning to Caroline, Vikram spoke in English. "Caroline, please do as I say just now. I know you have questions but hold them for the moment. I promise to answer them after we find a place to hide."

The sun dipped behind the mountains as Tashi led them down a steep slope. Unlike the Changthang plateau, where there was not a scrap of cover to hide behind, this section of Ladakh was deeply furrowed and mountainous. The ravines, gorges, cliffs, canyons and rock falls offered them hundreds of choices. Some distance down the slope Tashi led them into a cleft on the mountainside. It was so well hidden that Vikram walked past its narrow opening without noticing it.

"We come here sometimes to play," said Tashi as he led them along a narrow gully between vertical walls. The gully turned and ended beneath a rocky overhang. Tashi settled them below it.

"Nobody will find us here," asserted the boy confidently. "Even those who have been here often cannot find this place again."

Vikram wanted to sit in a corner and think but there was a look in Caroline's eyes that he could not ignore. He had a lot of explaining to do, and so, sitting down facing the girl, he began to talk.

It was nine in the evening and Aditya was sitting alone outside his tent, under the stars. It was cold and his gloved hands were buried deep in his jacket pockets.

Aditya was disturbed. Though the failure to make radio contact with Tina's group had not bothered Raghu or anyone else at the campsite, it troubled him. Raghu had shrugged it off, stating that unsuccessful attempts were common. Last time the batteries had run out. Their antenna could have broken or their machine might have malfunctioned; according to Raghu there could be several reasons for the breakdown. He had advised Aditya not to lose any sleep over the problem. If there was any genuine trouble somebody would have come across from Tina's camp and informed them about it. After all, the distance that separated the camps could be covered in two hours or less.

The routine post-dinner gathering and discussions were over, and after bidding each other goodnight, everyone had crawled into their sleeping bags. Only Aditya remained.

It was not just the lack of contact that perturbed Aditya. There was Anders's statement too. Anders had informed Aditya that his cook had disappeared the previous night. In the morning, when Aditya first heard of it, he had laughed at the incident. The agitated expressions on the faces of his Swedish friends had amused him no end. The disappearance of a cook from a campsite is a serious matter, since he is an indispensable member of an expedition. The cook's act of desertion could cut short the Swedish couple's trip. Raghu had put them at ease, however, saying that they were contributing well to the team effort and were welcome to stay on if they wished.

The cook's vanishing act had not bothered Aditya till he had had a conversation with Tsewang, the camp boy. That was at sunset. Aditya had wandered to the dining tent then for a cup of tea. Tsewang had served Aditya a steaming mug and he had chatted with the young Ladakhi. Their conversation had soon veered to the abrupt departure of Anders's cook.

"The cook was a strange man," Tsewang had said. "He kept asking me questions. The man wouldn't stop. He wanted to know where our second camp was and who were the people there. He enquired about all the expedition members and for some reason he was particularly interested in Tsering. He wanted to know how tall Tsering was, what he looked like and what languages he spoke. He was an exasperating man and I got fed up with his questions."

When Aditya asked Tsewang where the cook was from, Tsewang said that the man was from Tibet and that it was odd to see a Tibetan in these mountains.

After listening to Tsewang, Aditya had enquired further with Anders about his cook. "There was nothing wrong with him," the Swede had said. "He worked well and his food was good. But he was not the original man we had contracted to take with us." Anders had shaken his head in regret. "How I wish the first man had come. He was a good fellow but for some reason he backed out at the last moment and we were forced to bring this Tibetan man in his place."

Aditya was becoming increasingly uneasy. He had laughed at the cook's desertion in the morning, but now after hearing Anders and Tsewang's revelations, the man's sudden exit deeply troubled him. The cook was Tibetan, he had shown an unusual interest in Tsering and then he had disappeared.

Aditya decided that he needed to speak to Tsewang. He rose to his feet and walked towards the kitchen tent. Raghu, as was his wont, was listening to his radio. Faint crackles of hiss and static came from his tent as Aditya walked past. The rest of the tents were silent, their occupants fast asleep. Tsewang, however, was awake and Aditya found him sitting outside the kitchen tent carving a piece of wood with his penknife.

"Hullo, sir," grinned the boy when he saw Aditya.

"Hi, Tsewang, no I do not want tea," Aditya assured the boy when he rose to his feet. "I've come to talk to you. It is about the Tibetan cook. I want to know when he left from here. Was it last night or this morning?"

"Last night sir," replied Tsewang. "It was after dinner while everybody was asleep. I was in my sleeping bag and I heard a lot of movement. I didn't pay much attention then, but when I woke up the man was gone."

Aditya was silent. It was a day's walk to Leh. The man had left in the early hours of the night. He could have made it to Leh by morning. Could the cook be one of Akira's men? Akira was looking for them and Anders and Eva were a possible link to Vikram and him. Akira was desperate for leads and was the sort to explore every possible clue. Was it Akira who was behind the last-moment change of the original cook?

Aditya knew that he was stretching his imagination, but he was convinced that there was reason for doubt. An inquisitive Tibetan cook had gone missing in the morning and by evening a pre-arranged radio conversation had failed.

"What is the problem, sir?" asked Tsewang. "Something is worrying you, *saab*?"

"I am worried," admitted Aditya. "The silence from Tina's camp worries me. Why was there no reply?"

"I can go and check sir, their camp is not far."

"It's two hours away."

"Not for me, *saab*. I can get there in an hour's time. There are several paths to the camp. Some of these paths are difficult and Raghu *saab* will not take you that way. But I have grown up here and I have used these trails often. Should I go?"

Aditya looked at Tsewang. News from the other camp would set his mind at rest. But it wasn't fair to ask the boy to travel all that distance. Tsewang's daily workload was heavy and the boy needed his rest.

"Sir, I want to go to the other camp," persuaded Tsewang. "I want to meet my brother, Tashi. I promise to be back soon."

Permission to travel between camps had to be obtained from Raghu. But Aditya was not averse to bending rules. If Tsewang returned at a reasonable hour nobody would be aware of his little excursion.

"Are you sure you want to go?" asked Aditya.

Tsewang nodded, smiling broadly.

"Come back fast and wake me up when you return."

"Yes sir. Thank you, sir."

"Don't forget," reminded Aditya, wagging a finger. "First come to my tent, give me the news and *then* go sleep."

"Yes sir. Do not worry, sir."

Aditya returned to his tent feeling more at ease. It had been a tiring day, Tsewang could wake him when he got back.

Caroline's Story

The rock overhang cut off most of the sky, leaving only a glittering slice of stars visible. It was dark and cold in the shelter. The decision to carry his warm clothes with him that morning had not been easy for Vikram. Warm clothing is heavy and while climbing mountains every additional kilogram matters. Now, as the chill sharpened, he thanked his stars that he had resisted the temptation to leave the bulky clothing behind. Caroline had also carried the extra weight and she too was warm and snug. The cold did not bother young Tashi. Caroline and Vikram had offered him use of their clothing but he had refused, saying he was used to the cold. His patched and torn sweater was sufficient.

Caroline had looked expectantly at Vikram once they had settled as comfortably as was possible. Vikram was hesitant to start with. He was under oath not to reveal Tsering's identity, but he reasoned that under the circumstances he did not have a choice, especially if he wanted Caroline's co-operation. Caroline made it easy for Vikram by agreeing to his terms. Vikram made her promise not to repeat what he was about to disclose to anybody, not even her mother. Caroline listened in spellbound silence as Tsering's story unfolded. Tashi listened too, but because Vikram spoke in English, the boy did not follow much of what he said. Caroline absorbed every word and her eyes shone with wonder as Vikram narrated the mesmerising tale of Tsering's birth and eventful life.

"I'll be darned...our little Tsering...a lama? A reincarnated child?"

"He is a precious young boy and he obviously has an important role. That's why they want him, Caroline and *that* is the reason why we have to rescue him. Tsering's captors are holding him at Rumbak tonight. Later, when things have settled, Tashi and I are going to Rumbak to search for him. If we find him..."

"Tashi and you?" Caroline interrupted. "And what about me...? Vikram, don't you even for a moment think you can leave me out of this. Tsering is my friend too."

Vikram did not protest. He was glad that Caroline had offered to help; every extra hand was welcome. Caroline agreed with Vikram's plan to wait. A search party was prowling the mountains above. Lying low was the most sensible course of action. Two hours ought to be enough. The cold and dark should have turned them back by then.

Vikram questioned Tashi about trails to Rumbak. He did not want to use the regular trail as Akira might have placed lookouts along it. The man had been outwitted twice before and it was unlikely he would leave anything to chance this time. Tashi said that there was another less-used path through the mountains and he could lead them along it.

They still had time on their hands. At the magical meadow Caroline had begun talking about herself. Now in the lonely darkness she continued.

Her father was a wildlife lover. He had been a biologist and had worked for a zoo. Her mother, Julia, was an accountant. Caroline had treasured her childhood. Growing up with both her parents was the most memorable and wonderful period of her life. They had lived in Seattle, on the northwest coast of America. But all was not well at home. It started slowly with her mom and dad quarrelling. The quarrelling soon got worse and sometimes turned violent. It was horrible, she said, watching the two people she loved most in the world, say and do such terrible things to each other.

"I won't go into details, Vikram. All I need say is that their fighting tore my little world apart. The precious moments of my childhood ended abruptly when my mom walked out of the house one morning. My parents divorced and mom planned to move to Atlanta in Georgia. She wanted me to go with her but I refused, preferring to stay with daddy. Mom was terribly hurt by this, but I knew she was going there because she had found somebody else. She said that we could live together, the two of us and the new man in her life. They would both take care of me.

"How could I, Vikram? Daddy would be left all alone. I couldn't do that to him. Mom had somebody else, dad didn't. I sided with my dad and stayed back in Seattle. It was a terrible choice for a little girl to make. I was only nine years old then and I had to decide which parent I loved more. Mom was devastated and I don't know whether she has ever forgiven me for what I did. But then neither have I forgiven her for walking out on dad.

"The next part of my life was spent living with dad in Seattle. I missed mom terribly during those years and I think so did dad, but he never mentioned it. Mom would call often and she always sent me tickets to fly down to Atlanta during my holidays. But though I wanted to meet her I rarely went. I knew I was being mean, but I couldn't help it. I just couldn't bring myself to forgive her for what she had done. Pood dad...he never found anyone else.

"Over the years dad and I drew closer to one another. Our relationship was not just father and daughter; we became buddies. He was my most trusted friend. Those years with dad ended abruptly when he passed away in a freak accident two years ago. I was devastated – he was there one day and gone the next. The shock was terrible. Mom immediately flew down from Atlanta to look after me. She wanted me to give up everything in Seattle and go live with her, but I refused. I had lived my entire life in Seattle and I loved the place. All my friends were there and at that time I had a boyfriend too."

Vikram listened to Caroline without interrupting her. Her

words welled from deep within. It was the lonely solitude of their mountain refuge, thought Vikram. His father had told him that places like this had a strange effect on people. Caroline was sharing her most private feelings with him.

"Mom is a busy person. She runs a successful accounting firm. She had to go back to Atlanta and when she realised that I was not going to return with her, she left. I stayed alone in Seattle, but the place was not the same without dad. Till then I had never given a thought to how much I relied on him. He was the pillar of my life and I had leaned on him, taking his rock-like support for granted. My life began to crumble without him. I started doing badly at college and I fought with my boyfriend. We split up and that made things worse. I drifted, Vikram. I lost all direction and when that happens things quickly get out of hand. I found myself caught in a vicious downward spiral. I got into bad company and did things I should never have done. I led a terrible life for a year. I don't want to speak about it; all I can tell you is that it was the worst year of my life. A few months ago mom came and pulled me out of Seattle. I protested, I threw tantrums, but she stood firm, refusing to take no for an answer. She closed my place down and flew me to Atlanta.

"I was so bad that I needed rehabilitation. Mom took time off from work and sat beside me. I said horrible things to her, holding her responsible for all my problems. I yelled at her for ruining my life and happiness. At that time I needed someone to blame for the mess I had made of my life and mom was a convenient target. But despite it all she stayed by my side. After the rehab programmes were done with mom suggested that we go on a trip together. She was willing to take me anywhere I wanted to go. I remember being typically nasty and saying that I was not interested in going anywhere. I didn't bother to decide on a destination, but mom kept insisting.

"Then one day while cruising the internet I came across

a 'snow leopard' site. My father loved snow leopards deeply. They were his favourite animals at the zoo where he worked. He had single-handedly reared two cubs when their mother died. The cubs, Zara and Lara, were the other loves of his life, besides me." Caroline smiled in the dark. "They were the cutest things that you could ever set your eyes on; worthy competitors for dad's love."

"The website I found spoke about Raghu's snow leopard expedition. It said that its purpose was to study the snow leopard and its habitat. Those who participated in the expedition would learn about the ecology of the animal and their efforts and money would help Raghu with his work.

"Dad loved his snow leopards, Vikram, and the biggest regret of his life was his inability to ever see one in the wild. Dad was disabled in his left leg. The disability was not so serious that he could not move about on his own, but it was severe enough to prevent him from climbing mountains or trekking. It was extremely unfortunate. His experience with the cubs had made him a renowned authority on captive snow leopards, yet he would never be able to see them in the wild.

"From the moment I set eyes on Raghu's website I knew I had to do it for dad. The expedition Raghu offered was something dad would have dearly loved to be on. I wanted to contribute in my own little way to the study of the animal he loved, and live out his unachievable dream...the dream of seeing a snow leopard in the wild. Mom's eyes almost popped when I told her I wanted to go to Ladakh, in India. But when she realised that it was something to do with snow leopards she bought our tickets.

"I guess mom wanted to do this trip with me so that we could be together and become buddies — the way dad and I had been. But I made an awful mess of this expedition. I allowed myself to slip back to the horrible teenager I had been in Seattle. I hated everything in India and everybody here. Then I fell into the loo."

Vikram laughed and so did Tashi. Tashi's English was rudimentary and though he did not understand most of what Caroline said, 'loo', was a word he understood and the incident was one he remembered very clearly.

"I can laugh about it now," smiled Caroline ruefully. "But at that time I felt I could not have sunk any further. That morning, on that walk with you, Tsering and the others, I was in a trance. I remember that the mountainside we walked on was scary," Caroline shuddered. "I couldn't believe that Tina was taking us on such hair-raising paths. One wrong step and that would have been the end. As I walked along I often thought that falling off the mountain might not be too bad. It would have been a nice way to die. Goodbye mom, goodbye cruel world, goodbye rehab centres...hullo dad." Caroline swallowed. Her voice shook but she kept going. "Crazy things were going on inside my head. But when I found myself dangling on the edge of the cliff and my death wish about to be fulfilled, something snapped inside me. It was a wake up call. My life, everything I was, everything I wished to be, flashed before my eyes and I discovered that I did not want to die." Caroline shook her head. "The contradictions which sparred inside my head seem hilarious now. Just a few minutes earlier I would have been happy to fall off the mountainside, but then, when I was confronted with death, I didn't want to die. I desperately did not want to die." Caroline paused, her voice breaking.

Vikram was silent. He could sense that Caroline was deeply shaken.

Tashi could feel it too.

Vikram reached for Caroline's hand, linking his fingers with hers. Caroline's eyes glistened in the starlight. Holding tightly to his hand she moved closer to him.

"Come here, Tashi," she requested. When the boy settled next to her she held his hand too. "Those moments..." Caroline's voice quavered.

"When you were suspended in outer space," contributed Vikram helpfully.

"Yes," laughed Caroline. "Those moments when I floated in space changed my life. The experience jolted me...it smacked me hard and opened my eyes. I realised people cared for me. You, Vikram, a perfect stranger...despite my having bitten your ear off, you were risking your life for me."

"Don't remind me," said Vikram.

Caroline butted Vikram with her head. It was a gentle push. There was an intimate silence. Bonds of friendship were being forged in the lonely cave.

It was Caroline who broke the silence. "At first all I noticed in Leh were the power failures, the crummy hotels, the lousy plumbing and the terrible food. Now I remember the smiles on the peoples' faces, their warmth and their hospitality. The mountains appeared forbidding...I was frightened of them then. But the truth is that they are grand, infinitely beautiful..."

"How about awesome?" suggested Vikram.

"Yes, awesome if you like, Vikram. These mountains are awesome and so are their people. What strikes me about the people is their contentment. Look at Karma the horseman, or our cook, or even little Tashi here. Our Tashi is working a full-time job. He isn't even a teenager and he doesn't go to school. Yet, he always has a smile on his face. That's when I think about myself..."

"Spoilt brat," said Vikram without hesitation.

"Will you let me finish!" said Caroline exasperatedly. She butted Vikram once more before continuing. "Yes, spoilt brat is right. I am educated, young, have opportunities in life and the world is open to me, yet I made a mess of my life and blamed my mother for my problems. This trip has changed all that. It has taught me lessons I will never forget. There will never be a need for rehab centres for me again. I love my mother very dearly. I only hope she will forgive me."

Vikram squeezed Caroline's hand.

"It is not just your dangle in outer space that turned you around, Caroline," said Vikram. "I think travelling, moving out of your country, has also had an influence. My dad has always maintained that we live in sheltered cocoons. He says that travelling makes you see the world differently. It opens your eyes. We begin to ask questions about ourselves and the way we live. That is what happened to you when you saw how the people of Ladakh live and how they get by on so little and yet are happy. You questioned yourself Caroline, and you changed."

There was a thoughtful silence. For a long time no one spoke. Vikram did not enjoy the silence; his mind kept wandering to Tsering and the task ahead. Contemplation of the enormity and near impossibility of their mission only resulted in dejection and so Vikram, not wanting to further weaken his already tottering morale, picked up where Caroline had left off.

He spoke to Tashi. Caroline joined in too. They asked him about his home, his family, the animals his family possessed and how they lived out the long winters. Tashi told them about himself, his ambitions and his dreams of joining a prestigious unit of the Indian army called the 'Ladakh Scouts'.

The lonely intimacy of the cave had its effect on Vikram too. He found himself sharing his inner thoughts with his companions. He spoke about things which he never discussed with anyone else, not even Aditya. Caroline had opened her heart and now it was his turn. Vikram spoke about his mother. He fought back tears when he related her death and the terrible pain of her passing. He told them of his father; of how he had been a distant figure till then. When his mother died, his father had given up his job abroad and returned to their home to look after him. He spoke of the bonds that had formed between him and his father. His father had never demonstrated love before, but he had changed, adjusting to the role of being both a mother and a father. Vikram told them about his admission to a boarding school and how he had met Aditya.

Time flew by as they chatted. Caroline and Tashi appeared to have forgotten what the night held in store for them, but Vikram hadn't and kept glancing at his watch. The minutes ticked inexorably away and soon it was time to leave.

They silently collected their backpacks and slipped them on. The packs were heavy, filled with binoculars, telescopes and lunch boxes, things that were of no use to them now; but it was pointless leaving them behind. Hooding his torch with his hand Vikram inspected their stony retreat, making sure that they had collected all their belongings. He then slipped the torch into his jacket pocket and zipped it in safely.

They followed Tashi through the tunnel-like entrance of the overhang. There were clouds in the sky and their silvery tresses blotted the moon. Tashi guided them past towering mountain cliffs, choosing paths that took them through the deepest shadows. The going was tough. They stumbled often and sometimes fell to the ground. They grazed their shins, and skinned their hands. The torch would have eased their suffering, but Vikram avoided using it. They struggled up slopes and slid down valleys. Tashi pushed them hard. Sweat dripped from their bodies and their legs ached as they marched behind the young boy. As they negotiated a rock-strewn gully Vikram heard howling from above.

"*Shanku*," whispered Tashi.

Wolf! There were wolves up there, searching for prey. Were there snow leopards too, wondered Vikram?

They entered the Rumbak valley from its lesser-used end at the head of the valley. Fields and shadowy stone walls appeared indicating that the village was nearby. They came to a wide path with a stream of water flowing alongside it. The path led downwards, between the fields, towards the village.

Vikram entered a barley field. He squatted so that his head was below the level of the field wall. Caroline and Tashi settled themselves next to him.

After gathering his breath he turned to Tashi and addressed him in Hindi. "Tashi, listen carefully to me. We are going to wait for you while you first ascertain whether Tsering is here or not. If he is here, survey the house he is being held in. Count the number of guards you see and if any of your friends are awake, ask them how many people are inside. Find out whatever you can. But be careful, I expect that they would have posted guards at various places. Have an excuse ready in case somebody stops you. You are a local so they should believe whatever you say. Go and come back soon."

"Don't worry, *saab*," grinned Tashi as he departed. "I will look after myself and I will find out everything about Tsering."

There was no wind to rustle the barley. Its bamboo-like spikes stood like buried spears around them. Vikram was tense. It showed in the stillness of his expression and in the rigid manner he sat. Caroline too was uneasy. The time for soul-searching discussions was over. They sat in silence awaiting Tashi's return.

Two shadows emerged from the gloom some twenty minutes later. "This is my cousin, Lobsang," said Tashi introducing the second shadow.

Though it was not possible to see Lobsang's features Vikram guessed that he was young, about Tashi's age. He had curly hair and his teeth gleamed as he smiled.

"Tsering is here!" declared Tashi with a wide grin. "He is inside a house not far from this field. Lobsang and I went to look at the house before coming here. We couldn't get too close, because if we had, the two men on guard would have asked us questions. One man walks continuously around the house. I did not see the other, but Lobsang says he is there. He guards the entry to Rumbak village at the mouth of the valley. It is a good thing we did not enter from there. The man would have instantly spotted us." Tashi paused. "Vikram *saab*, rescuing Tsering is not going be easy. Besides the man who is continuously walking around the house, there are many other men. All of them are sleeping outdoors in the courtyard."

Vikram's shoulders drooped. But had he expected anything less? Had he not prepared himself for the worst? The odds were bound to be against them. It was up to him to accept the challenge and plan a successful strategy; rise above the odds.

Vikram turned to Lobsang. "Can you tell me more about the people who have abducted Tsering? When did they arrive? How many of them are there and do they have a Japanese man amongst them?"

"The men entered our village during the afternoon." Lobsang's voice was high-pitched like Tashi's. "I did not count them then but I am sure that there were at least ten of them. The Japanese man arrived later in the evening, with the boy. He is their leader and we were all surprised to hear him speak fluent Hindi and Ladakhi.

"We have many trekkers camping in our village and they are always welcome. But when we saw this group we instantly knew that they were not tourists. Two of them were armed and they made no effort to hide their weapons. We did not want the men to stay in our village but the Japanese man found old Dorje who lives alone in his house. He offered Dorje a large sum of money and the old man let them have his house for the night. Everybody hopes that these people will go away in the morning. Nobody wants them here."

"What did they say?" questioned Vikram. "Are they leaving in the morning?"

"Yes," replied Lobsang. "Dorje says that they are leaving tomorrow morning."

"Will someone please explain what's going on?" requested

Caroline exasperatedly. Excusing himself Vikram turned away from the boys and explained the situation to her.

"I don't know what's going on in your mind, Vikram," said Caroline after Vikram had spoken. "There are three of us, four if you include Lobsang. There are ten of them, two with guns. Do you really think you can rescue Tsering tonight?"

Vikram did not reply. He leaned against the cold stone wall and stared at the ground. Tsering had to be rescued, regardless of the odds stacked against them. And it had to be done tonight. Akira would be gone tomorrow.

Vikram closed his eyes. He considered his options, dwelling long on each one. Sneaking into the house was impossible; that was obvious after what Tashi and Lobsang had seen. It would be far-fetched to think that they could get past a sentry who was circling the house and also slip by an unknown number of men sleeping in the courtyard. It was clear that a direct rescue attempt was out of the question. Some kind of alternative strategy was required. The glimmerings of an idea had begun to surface in Vikram's head. At first, it seemed preposterous, but Vikram refused to discard it. He thought hard. It was a suicidal or, more correctly, a sacrificial plan. But as Vikram thought more about it the more convinced he became — desperate situations called for desperate measures.

Vikram asked Lobsang and Tashi a few more questions. He needed details of old Dorje's house. He wanted to know how many entrances it had and where in the house they thought Tsering might be imprisoned. Vikram listened intently to their answers and then disclosed his plan.

"You're mad!" exclaimed Caroline after Vikram had finished. "How can you sacrifice yourself? Do you have any idea of what they will do to you when they discover Tsering has escaped? They will thrash you, they might even kill you."

"There will be confusion if the plan works and Tsering escapes," countered Vikram. "I might be able to get away during that confusion. But that's not important Caroline, Tsering's safety is what matters."

Vikram overrode all protests. Did anybody have a better idea, he asked? He explained that the key to the success of his plan was the creation of a diversion. They had to somehow get everybody out of the house. If he succeeded in diverting Akira and his men, he would focus their attention on himself for as long as possible. The idea was to buy precious time so that Caroline and Tashi could sneak in and rescue Tsering. The biggest flaw in the plan was the fact that Vikram himself would certainly be captured. With this certainty in mind Vikram discussed what the others should do without him; where they were to take Tsering and the probable places to hide him. Vikram went over his plan again. Speaking alternately in English and Hindi he discussed every eventuality that could arise.

Caroline had stared disbelievingly at the schoolboy. How could Vikram plot his doom so calmly? She was upset, at first, at what she considered to be outright stupidity, but as Vikram spoke she slowly became convinced that under the circumstances, his plan made perfect sense. Vikram was thoroughly committed to Tsering's cause. She saw absolute selflessness, devotion and loyalty in her friend. In that cold barley field, under the moon and stars, her respect for Vikram multiplied boundlessly.

Captured

The moon rode high, free of its attendant clouds, and the Rumbak valley glowed a luminous silver under its light. Old Dorje's house, the one in which Tsering was imprisoned, lay in the cleft of the valley at Vikram's left. It was a typical two-storeyed Ladakhi house with a flat roof and a large courtyard. A stone fence encircled the house, clearly marking its boundaries. In the silvery darkness Vikram spotted two shadows near the front door. A few more were visible at one side of the house. There was no doubt in Vikram's mind that there were more shadows at the back of the house.

The shadows lay absolutely still. The men in the courtyard were fast asleep. However, one of them was awake; a sentry paced the walls of the courtyard. There was no set pattern to his movements. 'Paced' perhaps was not the correct word, because, in actual fact, the man was in no hurry at all. His gait could be better described as a shuffle. Studying the sentry as he wandered from wall to wall, Vikram estimated that he circuited the house once every three minutes.

Akira had fortified the house well. The sleepy plodding of the sentry did not deceive Vikram. He knew that it would be difficult to get past him. The men asleep in the courtyard were also positioned well. Breaking in was out of the question. Akira had secured every entrance. Tsering was locked away somewhere inside and Vikram was sure that Akira was sleeping nearby.

Vikram was sitting in a field, crouched behind its stone fence. Just beyond the fence trickled a stream. Vikram remembered it from his previous visit to Rumbak. At that time, under the heat of the blazing sun, the stream had flowed fast and furious. But now the glacier that fed the stream had frozen solid and the noisy stream was silent, its flow reduced to just a few feet in width.

On the far side of the wide stream bed lay Dorje's house and beyond the house were more stone walls and fields. Caroline and Tashi were in those fields. Vikram could not see his friends but he knew that they were hiding there.

Vikram had parted with the others after entering Rumbak village. While Caroline and Tashi had proceeded to their hiding place, Vikram and Lobsang had stolen silently towards Lobsang's home. Lobsang and his mother lived alone in a big house. His father worked in Leh and his brother was a monk at the Phyang monastery. Only his mother was in the house and she slept undisturbed as they entered. Lobsang seated Vikram in the dark living room and brought him some paper and a pen. Vikram then wrote a letter by candlelight. On completing it he carefully folded it and handed it to Lobsang. After a short discussion with the boy Vikram departed for the fields.

The houses in Rumbak village were set far apart, some amidst fields and others beside the stream bed. Not a sound had come from the village as he passed through it. Everyone was fast asleep. Just one person seemed to be awake in Rumbak and that was the sentry.

Lobsang's home was visible from where Vikram crouched. It was set back amongst the fields towards the head of the valley. Because he knew that the Ladakhi boy was sitting at the doorstep he discerned a shadow there. Vikram glanced at the sentry and confirmed that he was not looking his way. He then rose quickly and waved to Lobsang.

This was the signal for Lobsang to proceed. The boy rose to his feet and started forward. Stepping out of his house, he walked unconcernedly along the stream bed. There was no need for him to hide. He had been instructed to walk over to the sentry and hand him a note that was to be delivered to Akira.

The sentry only noticed Lobsang when the boy walked up to the gate. Vikram saw the man jerk upright and then stagger forward. His sudden, clumsy advance disturbed the men sleeping near the door of the house and they sat up in their sleeping bags. Vikram kept his fingers crossed as he watched Lobsang talk to the sentry at the gate. The men who had woken gathered inquisitively around the sentry.

The note was the key to Vikram's plan. He breathed a sigh of relief when one of the men, after staring at the note for a long time, turned and walked to the house. Barely a minute later a light appeared in one of the upstairs rooms. Vikram clenched his fist.

The note had been delivered to Akira!

Vikram had written the note as carefully and as neatly as was possible in the flickering light of Lobsang's candle. The message was short.

Mr. Akira Singh,

I, the writer of this note, am standing not far from the house in which you have chosen to spend the night. I know you have the young lama Tsering in your custody but it is not about him that I wish to speak to you. Something has happened at the camp from which you abducted the boy. I am sure you are interested in ascertaining the events. If you come to the gate, I shall walk down and discuss the matter with you.

A friend.

Vikram had intentionally used Akira's full name. It would be a shock for him to discover that somebody in this remote corner of Ladakh was aware of his identity. The idea was to unnerve Akira. The contents of the note were vague and confusing and though it prompted questions, it provided no answers. Vikram extracted his binoculars from his pack and pressing them to his eyes he stared at the door. Would Akira take the bait and step out? The minutes dragged slowly past and just as Vikram was beginning to worry, the door opened and four men walked out. The moonlight was sufficient for him to see their features. The first three were strangers but the lines of the fourth were instantly recognisable. There was no mistaking the curly hair, the flat cheeks and the long angular body. Akira had bitten the bait.

Vikram surveyed the courtyard, counting the men within it. Had he managed to draw all the men out? There were ten men in the courtyard. Yes! The note had had the desired effect. The men were clustered near the gate and Akira was standing next to Lobsang, talking to the Ladakhi boy.

Vikram tucked his binoculars carefully into his backpack. Abandoning his backpack in the field he rose and pulled himself over the fence. He was instantly spotted by the gathering at the gate and all attention was directed to him. This was exactly what Vikram wanted. Tashi could make his move now.

Caroline and Tashi were hiding in the fields behind Dorje's house. From where they sat they couldn't see the front gate of the house; instead they had a view of the backyard and the back-facing rooms.

They had seen Lobsang set off from his house. They anxiously followed his movements as he walked along the stream bed. But he soon disappeared behind the walls of the house and with the gate blocked from view they did not witness what transpired there.

"Akira's room," Caroline whispered when a candle was lit in one of the rooms on the upper floor. They soon noticed movement all around the house and torches beamed inside the compound. Shadows which had been lying inert in the backyard rose to their feet and crossed to the front gate. The sentry no longer made his rounds.

Vikram's diversion was proving to be successful. The backyard had emptied like magic. Though the coast appeared clear for Tashi, Caroline held the boy back. The windows of the candlelit room overlooked the backyard. She could see people inside it, as the candlelight threw several shadows against its walls. Caroline held Tashi's hand.

Caroline was certain that the candlelit room was Akira's. He and his cronies were probably wondering what to make of Vikram's note. After several minutes the shadows trooped out of the room and the candle burned unattended.

"*Go*!" whispered Caroline.

Tashi sprang to his feet. He was aware that time was precious. Vikram had bought him a few minutes. There was no telling how long Vikram could hold their collective attention; every second counted.

"Best of luck," whispered Caroline. "Come back with Tsering. I shall wait here for you."

Tashi slipped over the stony field fence and crouched when he landed on the other side. The way was clear for him. Keeping low he ran toward Dorje's fence. Moonlight betrayed Tashi's presence. He would have been spotted by anybody looking in his direction. Vikram had been right, thought Caroline; his diversion was crucial. No other plan would have got them even close to Tsering.

Tashi disappeared for a moment when he jumped Dorje's backyard fence and ducked below it. He was now inside the compound. Caroline saw him again when he ran to the rear wall of the house.

Tashi and Vikram had concluded earlier that it was too dangerous to enter the house from the ground floor. The safest point of entry was from the top, via the terrace. The house had two floors and Vikram had asked Tashi how he would climb to the top. Tashi had said that it was easy to get up there and Caroline could see why. Ladakhi villagers build their houses slowly. The ground floor is completed first and rooms on the floor above are added only when money is available. Though Dorje had plans of completing all his rooms, one remained incomplete. The room was an empty platform at the level of the first floor.

Caroline watched Tashi edge along the house wall. The missing room was at the rear of the house. Tashi positioned himself below the room and leapt. His grasping fingers caught hold of the platform above and he yanked himself up, as if performing a pull-up, till his body cleared the platform and he raised a leg on to it. There were steps at the far end, leading to the terrace. Tashi climbed them, crawling on his hands and knees. Caroline saw him pause when his head cleared the terrace level. Tashi flattened himself as he emerged on the terrace, dragging himself along its rough surface. Like all Ladakhi houses this one too had an entrance on its roof and it was from there that Tashi planned to enter the house.

Vikram walked slowly towards Dorje's house. The gathering at the gate followed his every move as he forded the stream. Vikram took his time, pausing to locate dry rocks on which he could step across. He managed to cross without getting his feet wet and then walked confidently forward.

He halted outside Dorje's gate. Akira was staring at him. Although he had just woken, his eyes were alert, gazing expectantly at Vikram.

"You woke me from my sleep," began Akira. His English was faintly accented.

"We have met before," said Vikram.

"Yes we have, I remember you."

Vikram was silent.

"How do you know my name?" Akira's tone had changed. It was aggressive now.

"You were born in Hong Kong," said Vikram.

Akira's facial muscles contracted.

Vikram had his attention. "Your father is Indian and your mother Japanese. You are an international smuggler and you have specialised in smuggling along the Ladakh-China border." Vikram paused.

"Go on!" It was an order.

Akira's men looked on silently. Vikram wondered how many of them could follow what he was saying.

"You have been smuggling tiger bones across the border. You deliver them in Chinese-Tibet and collect shahtoosh in return. Trade in this item is banned in India, yet you carry it to Srinagar. You employ your own weavers in the city." Vikram was fabricating now. "They weave you fabulous shahtoosh shawls and you clandestinely slip these out of India and sell them in western markets where they fetch you enormous sums of money." Vikram paused again.

"Go on," repeated Akira.

Vikram continued. He now spoke about Tsering. Everyone was listening to him; he had their attention. It was up to Tashi now.

Tashi carefully pushed aside the plank of wood which covered the entrance into the house. There were steps descending to the upper floor. A dim, flickering light pitched shadows across a large hall. The hall was empty. Tashi crept down a couple of steps, then halted and carefully rearranged the plank of wood above his head.

Having grown up in Rumbak, Tashi was familiar with the interiors of all its homes. He knew every room in Dorje's house. On his left were three doors. One led to the kitchen, the next opened into a sitting room, and behind the third was a candlelit prayer room. In the centre of the hall were steps that led down to the ground floor.

Tashi thought it unlikely that Tsering was imprisoned in any of the rooms to the left. On his right, beyond the walled-off, unfinished room were two additional rooms.

The first was the candlelit one that Akira had chosen to sleep in. The door beyond it was locked.

It was behind this door that Tashi suspected Tsering was being held. On light feet he hurried to the door. This was Dorje's store-room. It was always empty because Dorje had a more convenient one below. Tashi looked down at the solid steel latch which was bolted in place by a large padlock. Tashi knocked softly against the door. At first there was silence; then Tashi heard movement.

"Tsering!" he whispered.

"Tashi!" came the reply from behind the door.

Tashi's hands pulled at the latch. Using all his strength he tugged at it, but the latch refused to yield. Tashi quickly realised that he did not possess the strength to break it open. But the store-room had only one entrance – to rescue Tsering he would have to open this door. He needed to find the key to the lock.

"Tsering, I cannot open the door. I need the key," he whispered, "Do you know where it is?"

"Akira," replied Tsering.

"Wait."

On tiptoe Tashi stole to Akira's room. The door was open and in the faint candlelight his eyes flitted across the room. The only furniture was a bed, a table and a chair. There were no keys on the table or the bed. Akira's rucksack was on the ground. Clothes lay scattered near it. It would take time to search Akira's belongings. Tashi breathed deeply. He glanced at the hall and down the stairs. The house was silent; Vikram was still holding their attention. With a determined stride he entered the room and stooped beside the rucksack.

Standing at the front gate Vikram talked at length about Tsering. He then spoke about 'Nirvana Travels' and its fat, bespectacled owner. Akira's henchmen, despite not understanding what was passing between Vikram and their boss, continued to stand around the gate. They were curious about Vikram. They wanted to learn more about this boy who had managed to draw their boss out of his sleep.

Soon Vikram found himself running out of topics that would interest Akira and it was with relief that he welcomed the kidnapper's questions. When queried about how he had obtained his information, Vikram responded with an explanation of the international concern for the diminishing numbers of Tibetan antelope. He also spoke about the efforts to stop tiger poaching. Vikram's father was at the forefront of the battle against the poachers who threatened the survival of these species and so Vikram could speak eloquently and knowledgeably about these subjects.

"Your problem, Mr. Akira, is that by dealing in products from endangered species you have attracted the attention of powerful international organisations. These organisations have the resources and the ability to track you down and they have begun to do so. Their investigations have led them to Leh already. If you return to Leh it will be at considerable risk. Your exit from this country will be difficult too. They have placed a detention order on your passport."

"I have several passports, my friend," said Akira contemptuously. "I have been in this business for many years. I have a number of sources of information here and I know exactly what is happening in Leh. I was aware of Mr. Reddy's visit and I know that they are searching for me."

"There is no need for me to return to Leh." A smile played on Akira's lips. "I leave Ladakh tomorrow. My exit will be spectacular, it will be in a manner your friends and investigating authorities will never dream of. Your so-called 'international agencies' have been tracking me for years. I have always kept a step ahead of them and I shall continue to do so. Your little lecture about endangered species does not cut any ice with me. Don't for a moment think that I will be persuaded to stop dealing in shahtoosh and tiger bones."

"Why?" interrupted Vikram agitatedly. "What right do we have to destroy these species and wipe them off the face of this planet? Why don't you give them a chance? Leave them alone! They too have a right to live!"

"Don't try and teach me what is right and what is wrong, my young friend. It is not I who is killing these animals. I am simply a businessman. There are millions of people who want medicines made from tiger bones. There are thousands who want to own the fabulous shahtoosh shawls. These people need my services and are willing to pay huge sums of money for these items. Like any successful businessman I supply what people want. If I do not supply them, they will get the goods from somebody else. I don't use tiger bone medicines and I personally don't care for shahtoosh shawls. Get it clear in your head that it is not Akira who is driving these animals to extinction. It is those *educated* people with money in their pockets who are responsible. Your 'international organisations' have got it all wrong. Tell them to stop wasting their time and money following me – it is pointless. If they catch me, someone else will take my place. You arrest him, and somebody else will take his place. The killing will go on. Tell your precious organisations to focus on the *cause* of the problem. Their money can be better spent on educating people not to use tiger bone medicine and not to aspire for shahtoosh shawls."

"How can you say 'businessman'?" protested Vikram. "How can you wipe away the blood of all these animals by simply saying that your trade is a 'business?' If there weren't people like you there would be no business." So strong was Vikram's feeling for the tiger and the helpless Tibetan antelope that he forgot the purpose of his confrontation with Akira. His righteous indignation blinded him and the exit of one of Akira's men from the surrounding cluster escaped him. The man turned and headed for the house.

Tashi did not see the man either. He was busy searching Akira's room for the keys to the padlocked room. The candlelight had betrayed Tashi. The man had noticed suspicious movement amongst the shadows on the upstairs walls. He was much larger than Tashi and he grabbed the prying boy by the scruff of his neck. Lifting him bodily, he carried Tashi down the stairs.

The first Vikram spotted of his friend was when Tashi was thrust unceremoniously in front of Akira. The kidnapper was nonplussed. He looked blankly at Tashi, not understanding the reason for the fuss, but then he saw the shock on Vikram's face.

"So," said Akira with a grim smile. "So this is the reason why I was pulled out of my bed." He saw Vikram look desperately about him. "Don't even for a moment think of trying to get away, young man. My men will run you down. I have a gun in my pocket. Do not tempt me to use it."

Akira casually unsheathed his weapon and at a signal from him, his men formed a circle around Vikram.

A horrified Caroline had witnessed Tashi's capture in Akira's room. She shook as the enormity of the catastrophe sank in. They would capture Vikram too and she would be all alone. Vikram's sacrifice was going to be in vain. Tsering's fate was sealed. Caroline bowed her head and fought her tears. She had to control her despair. Her freedom was her friends' final hope. Breaking down now would betray that last hope.

Caroline took a vow. Squatting amidst the strands of barley she promised herself that she was going to do whatever it took to help her friends. She was not going to walk away from this one, even if it exposed her to danger and possible capture. She breathed deeply, combating the dizziness that threatened to overpower her. She clamped her eyes shut and shook her head.

"Think!" Caroline demanded of herself. The kidnappers

would have realised by now that Vikram's note was nothing but an attempted diversion. It was a trick, a ruse to permit Tashi to sneak into the house. They would soon return to the house and to their beds to continue their interrupted slumber. Would the men let down their guard now that the rescue attempt had failed? Would they do away with the patrolling sentry? Caroline could only guess. But she couldn't afford to ignore the possibility that they would return to their former positions and make it impossible for her to sneak in.

There was no one in the backyard at the moment. Her path to the roof was clear. Caroline rose unhesitatingly to her feet and jumping the field wall she ran towards the house. No one saw her leap the backyard fence or drag herself to the level of the unfinished room. Following the same route Tashi had taken, she climbed to the terrace. Lying flat on its surface she wiggled her way to the central entrance. Reaching out for the wooden plank that covered the entrance, she shifted it, creating a tiny opening, sufficient to look down through.

Disaster

Akira was in an effusive mood. Vikram and Tashi were seated on the ground opposite him in Dorje's sitting room. The room was tastefully decorated and its wooden floor was carpetted. There were several chairs and couches scattered about. Three large candles and a kerosene lantern burned in the room. Five of Akira's men were in the room too, all clutching glasses filled with the local Ladakhi beer called *chang*. Neither Vikram nor Tashi's hands were tied but the presence of two more men lurking in the doorway squashed any hopes of their breaking away.

Akira's relaxed, complacent expression clearly conveyed that he thought his troubles were over. The kidnapper admitted his relief to Vikram.

"You and your friend, the tall boy, have given me enough trouble." Akira took a long swig from his glass. "But for your interference, this operation would have been completed a long time ago. You were schoolboys; I underestimated you and that was my mistake. I should have supervised the first operation at Tso Kar myself. Unfortunately, I left it in the hands of my people and all of you, including the Swedes, escaped to Leh." Akira leaned forward. "Tsering is worth a lot of money to me," he continued. "He is worth more than five years' profits in the wildlife trade. You boys frustrated me. I was so desperate to find Tsering in Leh that at one stage I even considered abducting the two of you and forcing you to lead me to him."

"We couldn't have helped you," said Vikram. "We had no idea where he was."

"Yes, but how was I to know that? At the time you two were my only leads to Tsering. Your abduction was carefully planned. I would have kidnapped you if it weren't for an absolute stroke of luck. Tsering suddenly showed up at Phyang village. I have friends in Phyang and they informed me of his presence. I captured the boy once more and this time I was convinced that everything was over, but I didn't take into account your friend, Aditya. I must admit he made fools of us. He took us by surprise and vanished without a trace."

Akira paused to refill his glass. "Both of you disappeared as though the mountains had swallowed you. I traced your Colonel Chacko. I trailed your friends Dolma and the Swedish couple. I questioned your hotel boys but nobody knew where you two had gone. It was eventually your Swedish friends who led me to you. When I discovered that they were going on a trek I arranged for a change in their cook. It was a shot in the dark but I was desperate enough to follow every possible lead. The cook recognised your friend Aditya. I had photographed the two of you at Leh and he was carrying copies of the prints. He talked to the camp boy and found out that you and Tsering were at the other camp. My man deserted the camp last night and reached Leh this morning. We travelled here immediately. Capturing the boy was easy, but your absence worried me. I expected trouble tonight and rightly so. Yours was a clever trick young man, but it didn't work."

Akira leaned back. "Your tall friend still worries me. I had wanted to take over his camp too, but I don't have enough men. Although I believe that they have no idea of what has happened, I am not going to repeat past mistakes. Guards will be maintained around the house and all three of you will be safely locked away."

Akira smiled at Vikram and then yawned. He glanced at his men. They were boisterously cracking loud jokes. He looked at his watch and then at his bottle. It was late but there was time for one more drink. Victory was at hand; a little celebration couldn't hurt.

Refilling his glass he turned to the boys again. "I can afford a long holiday after this operation. I won't need to do any smuggling for quite some time. The money from this assignment is excellent and I will be able to sit back and enjoy myself for many years. My temporary retirement will lessen the tiger bone trade, I'm sure. My absence will be a setback for the poachers, but that's good isn't it? There could be a respite for tigers. You might not believe what I say, but the fact is that I like animals too."

"I'm sure you do," mocked Vikram. "Your love for animals is as genuine as my love for kidnapping."

"Seriously," said Akira earnestly. "I have always liked animals. I have visited all the sanctuaries of this country...I have been to Kanha, Kaziranga, Ranthambore and Corbett. Dealing in animal products doesn't mean that I do not appreciate the creatures. I believe that people should be clear about their priorities, like I am. I am fond of animals. But I will not let that override my business instincts. Money is important. I'm willing to pursue any job as long as the money is good."

"Even kidnapping of young lamas?" questioned Vikram bitterly.

"Don't talk rubbish Vikram. I expect more sense from you...I was beginning to respect you. You and your friend Aditya are both tough kids who made me work hard for my money. I admire your fighting instincts. Don't spoil it all by talking about morals. Morals are conveniences to make you feel good. Don't get fooled by them. Listen carefully to me, Vikram. I am telling you this because I like you. The secret of my success is my hard work and diligence. If you want to succeed in life, work hard, plan and use your brains. But that's not all. Execution of your plans has to be perfect and for that you have to be ruthless. Never let complications like what is right and what is wrong come in your way. These things do not matter. What matters is success, triumph and money. Always strive to win – using any means, fair or foul – and like me you will be a rich man one day."

Vikram thought it unwise to pursue the argument. This was not the time to point out how warped the values being presented to him were. Akira had already downed several glasses of *chang*. Reasoning with him just now could have dangerous consequences.

Akira's cheerful mood persisted and he placed an arm around Vikram as he personally led the boys to the store-room. "I am gone tomorrow," he said, smiling. "The boy and I. We shall depart first thing in the morning. It's all over."

"It's not over," asserted Vikram defiantly, standing beside the store-room door. "Not till you make it to Tibet. They are waiting for you back in Leh. Every border post and every airport has been warned about you."

"I like you, Vikram," said Akira with a big smile. "You have spirit. You are a fighter to the bitter end." Akira pulled off his gloves. He reached into his jacket pocket and brought out a large key. "This is the key that your friend was searching for. Your plan was doomed from the start. The key is always with me. I never let it out of my sight. The little boy is too precious, he is my gold."

"You can lock me away," said Vikram as Akira slipped the key into the lock. "It doesn't matter because there are others who will get you."

"Who?" asked Akira turning. "Your friend Aditya? Uh-huh. There are guards in place between Rumbak and his camp, and my men will be sleeping in the courtyard. Nobody is going to stop me. I will be gone first thing in the morning. Nobody, not even your friends in Leh, will be able to do anything about it. Let me show you why."

Akira spoke in Tibetan to one of his men who turned and hurried to his room. The man returned shortly with a leather bag which he handed to his boss. Akira clicked it open and withdrew a dark object that looked like a thick version of a standard cordless phone.

Vikram saw excitement in Akira's eyes. There was child-like enthusiasm in the kidnapper's voice as he spoke. "You see this?" he asked, holding up the instrument like a proud schoolboy showing off his toy. "This is a satellite phone. It allows you to make a call from anywhere in the world. Right now, sitting here in Rumbak where there are no telephone or mobile connections, I can call anyone, anywhere on this planet." Akira's eyes gleamed as he stared at the instrument in his hand. "I have always wanted to possess one of these, but earlier these phones were large, unwieldy contraptions. Now they are a convenient size, almost as handy and small as mobile phones. This phone, Vikram, is invaluable to a person like me. Last evening, after capturing Tsering I made a call from your campsite to arrange for a helicopter. The aircraft will be here by eight in the morning and the boy and I will be gone."

Vikram swallowed.

"Ha! Ha!" laughed Akira, seeing Vikram's crestfallen face. "You have no answer; nobody has an answer to this master stroke of mine. This little gadget is indeed priceless. It took me just five minutes to organise my escape."

"You won't get far," said Vikram bravely. "Ladakh airspace is restricted and the Air Force will get you in no time."

"Vikram..." Akira shook his head. "Don't take me for a fool. Never underestimate your enemy, it is the worst mistake you can make. Everyone knows that Ladakh airspace is restricted. However, I also know that tourist flights with prior permission are permitted. I had made an application and had booked a helicopter some time ago. My application states that I need an aircraft for the purpose of heli-skiing, and since this is a valid request, the application was passed. I had paid the money for the helicopter flight before I left Leh. My phone call was only to arrange the time and place for the pick-up. I shall be collected from here and ferried to a snow-covered mountain. Don't bother to ask me where

I'm going or what I plan to do once I get there. Both Tsering and I will disappear. That will be the last anyone shall see of us."

Akira opened the store-room door and the boys were shepherded in.

Tsering embraced Vikram and Tashi as soon as they stepped in.

"Don't worry yourself too much," comforted Akira as he closed the door. "You and Aditya have done well. You have lost this battle but there will be others for you to fight. Sleep tight, I'll see you in the morning."

The latch was bolted and the lock clicked into place.

Caroline had heard every word that Akira said. His loud voice carried easily across the hall and through the opening she had created for herself. Lying flat on the terrace she kept her eye pressed against the slit-like crack. The store-room door was visible. Two men stood around Vikram and Tashi while Akira talked, squashing any hopes of escape. Caroline saw Akira lock the boys and place the store-room keys in his jacket pocket. Then standing at the landing, he issued instructions to his men. She heard footsteps descending the stairs and another set walking in her direction. Caroline panicked. She shrank away from the entrance. Bales of straw had been heaped on one side of the terrace. Caroline scurried towards the straw and squeezed herself between the terrace wall and the hay. She had barely concealed herself when the wooden cover of the terrace was pushed aside.

Footsteps mounted the terrace. Caroline held her breath as the footsteps moved forward. She cringed when she heard a voice speak loudly. Another voice replied from the courtyard below. Caroline's numbed brain informed her that the voice from the terrace was Akira's. He was talking to his men below in the courtyard. He had not spotted her. But for some reason she was convinced that Akira was looking for her and that it was only a matter of time before he would find her. Caroline lay absolutely still, waiting for the inevitable. Soon, she heard footsteps again. This was followed by the sound of the wooden lid of the terrace being dragged back into place. The footsteps descended and then there was silence.

Akira had gone!

Caroline's throat quivered and she trembled with relief. The straw had saved her. Akira was not looking for her, but only checking on his men below. Caroline lay motionless for a long time. The cold dug into her cheeks and froze them, but she barely noticed. It did not strike her that the clouds which had dogged the moon had disappeared, and that the sky was clear. The westward passage of a million heavenly bodies was lost on her. It was a spectacular streak of light which shot across the sky that jolted her to her senses. Caroline gasped. That was by far the most brilliant shooting star she had ever seen in her life. It was quickly followed by two lesser streaks that momentarily sparked the great darkness above. Caroline stirred. Despite the insulating effect of the hay her body was frozen. She shivered uncontrollably for several minutes before rising and regaining control of herself.

The house was silent. She crawled to the edge of the terrace and peered over the wall. In the moonlit courtyard below, Caroline spotted several shadows. Two men were sleeping beside the entrance door. Another two slept beneath the back wall. There were many sleeping bags below one of the sidewalls, but the other wall was empty — no one slept below it. This wall faced the head of the valley, from where a strong wind blew. It was the bitter cold of the wind that had discouraged the kidnappers from resting there.

No sentry patrolled the grounds.

If she was to escape, the windy, unguarded side of the house was her only avenue. Caroline crept towards the windward wall and peered over its edge, looking down. She was two floors above the ground – too high to jump. But a ledge ran across the wall above the first floor, jutting out a few inches. If she hung herself from the terrace wall she could drop safely on to the ledge. From there it was just a single-floor jump to the ground.

The ledge offered a feasible escape route. She could jump down, cross the stream and escape into the mountains. Caroline looked up at the mountains. They were black, steeply rising shadows. Their smooth outlines crowded around the Rumbak valley like dark prison walls. She would head for the mountains soon, she thought. She would seek shelter within them...she and her friends. She knew where her friends were imprisoned and she knew where the keys to their prison were. All that was necessary was to effect their rescue.

Her only obstacle was Akira. The guards in the courtyard were asleep. She had to wait till Akira fell asleep too. Caroline decided to allow a half-hour to pass before entering the house. There was no need to hurry. Tsering's freedom was at stake. The price of a mistake was unthinkable.

Thirty minutes and two shooting stars later, Caroline crouched beside the wooden plank. She lifted it slowly and gently pushed it aside. Candles burned in the hall. There was no sound. Caroline lowered her head, inserting it through the opening. In the flickering light she scanned the hall. It was empty.

Caroline carefully placed her foot on the first step. Beads of sweat gathered on her forehead as she concentrated on each step, soundlessly placing her feet on each stair. The beads turned to a flood by the time she reached the landing. Soft light emerged from the prayer room. Three additional candles glimmered quietly outside the living room, eerily lighting the hall. Caroline crouched so as to reduce the length of her shadow.

Loud snores floated up from the ground floor. Caroline listened carefully; there was no sound of movement. The door to Akira's room was ajar. Caroline crept towards it. She paused at the door and heard steady, even breathing from within. She inched herself across the doorway. Akira had stretched his sleeping bag on the bed and was asleep inside it. He was sleeping face up, nose pointing to the ceiling. Caroline spotted Akira's jacket hanging from a peg on the wall.

The opening between the door and its frame was wide enough for Caroline to pass through. She entered the room on her knees. Her feet sensed a rug beneath her as she crept forward. There was no break in Akira's breathing as she rose to her feet below the peg. Her hands glided over the jacket. Finding a pocket she probed it with her fingers. No keys. There was something hard and metallic in the next pocket. Caroline felt the unmistakable shape of a key. Carefully extracting it she crouched again. She then soundlessly retraced her path out of the room.

Caroline did not pause to savour her success. She crept directly to the store-room. The key fitted the lock and there was a faint click when she turned it. With utmost care she unbolted the latch and pushed the door. Stepping into the room she closed it behind her.

"Vikram," she whispered.

"Caroline!"

The darkness within was absolute and Caroline could not see anything. "Is Tsering here?" she questioned.

"Yes, Caroline sister." A small hand reached out and touched her. Caroline held the hand and pulled gently. She hugged Tsering fiercely. Tears collected in her eyes.

"Caroline..." it was Vikram.

Caroline reached out and embraced him. "You and your crummy diversion," she whispered in his ear.

Vikram smiled in the darkness and squeezed her hand. "It was worth saving you up in the mountains," he whispered. "I ...ouch."

Caroline had pinched him.

"Let's get out of here," said Vikram, holding her hand. "Which way did you come, Caroline? From the roof or from downstairs?"

"The roof."

"Do we go back that way?"

"Yes."

"You and Tashi wait here. I'll take Tsering first. You follow once we reach there, is that okay?"

"Sure."

"Silence everybody, I'm opening the door."

Vikram gently pushed the door and holding Tsering's hand he stepped out. Vikram crouched and crawled forward, showing Tsering the way. Reaching the stairs he climbed them and stepped on to the terrace. Tsering joined him soon after. Caroline and Tashi arrived a minute later. Having looked down from each of the four walls, Vikram, like Caroline, decided on the windward wall, below which no one slept. Caroline found him there staring at the ledge below.

"We'll have to jump onto that ledge," whispered Caroline. "It's the only possible way out of here."

"Yes, but what about Tsering and Tashi? They cannot jump that distance."

Vikram was right. She and Vikram were tall enough to lower themselves onto the ledge. But Tashi and Tsering were too short and their legs would dangle well above the narrow band of cement.

"You go first, Caroline. Cross the wall and wait for us in the fields. I will lower myself next and stand on the ledge and help both of them down."

The plan made sense to Caroline; Vikram could help both the boys down. She mounted the wall and holding on to its edge she lowered herself along it. At full stretch her shoes rested on the ledge below and she slowly transferred her weight from her hands to her feet. The ledge was a little more than six inches wide and she turned gingerly on it.

Vikram watched as the girl crouched and jumped the final twelve feet to the ground.

There was an audible thud when Caroline's feet hit the ground. Not moving, she sensibly remained where she was. She waited a full minute before rising and crossing the wall. Vikram saw her ford the stream and settle herself in the field.

Vikram explained his plan to Tsering and Tashi. He told them that he would wait on the ledge and help each of them down. He then lowered himself, but he was not as tall as Caroline and his feet did not touch the ledge, even at full stretch. He was lucky to maintain his balance when he transferred his weight to his legs.

"Tsering," he whispered. "You first."

Facing the wall the little lama lowered himself. Vikram reached up and held him. Tsering let go of the wall and transferred his weight to Vikram. Vikram felt a tremor beneath him. The ledge...

"Oh no!" he breathed.

Was the ledge going to collapse under their combined weight? Thankfully the support held while Vikram quickly turned Tsering around and lowered him. Vikram hurriedly let go and the boy landed safely, with a less audible thud than Caroline's. Tsering rose and ran silently to the wall. Vikram waited till Tsering had settled himself beside Caroline in the field. He then looked up. Tashi had already begun to lower himself. Vikram reached up and grasped the boy. When Tashi transferred his weight to Vikram's hands the ledge crumbled without warning.

The Wall

There was no time for either of them to prepare for the fall. Tashi slipped from Vikram's grip as they plummeted to the ground. Vikram somehow managed to bunch his knees below him as he fell. Landing on his feet he rolled to lessen the impact.

Vikram had taken the fall well but Tashi had not. Vikram saw the boy writhe in pain beside him. The sound of their combined fall, together with the crash of crumbled masonry, exploded like thunder in the silence of the night.

Vikram heard voices as he rose to his feet. Akira's men had been alerted. Tashi was in no state to rise. Vikram reached down and lifted the boy. Tashi was lightly built and Vikram managed to run despite the weight of the boy.

Reaching the wall Vikram placed Tashi on it. The young Ladakhi was in terrible pain. He had smashed his hands and knees during the fall, yet the boy gritted his teeth and swung himself over the wall, landing painfully on the other side. Vikram jumped and dropping beside the boy he reached out to lift him again.

"No!" cried Tashi. "I cannot run. Forget about me, I will hide in the village. You go!"

Vikram looked in desperation at Tashi. They were both crouching beneath the courtyard wall, out of sight from the people inside. "Come on," he implored. "I can carry you."

"No!" exclaimed Tashi. "I cannot. The pain is terrible. You don't understand. You go, leave me!" Tashi forced the decision on Vikram by turning and scrabbling away from him.

"Tashi!" cried Vikram in anguish.

But there was no going back now. It was too late. There was loud shouting from the house. With a final despairing glance at Tashi, Vikram turned and ran. But Vikram did not run towards Caroline and Tsering. They were safe in the fields; no one had spotted them. Revealing their location to the kidnappers was senseless. Instead, Vikram decided to lead the men away from his friends. He ran to the field, but he ran to a point far south of the spot where his friends were hiding.

Vikram splashed across the stream, not feeling its freezing waters. The sound of running feet behind him did not surprise him. Reaching the field wall, Vikram ran along it, steering his pursuers away from Tsering and Caroline. Glancing back, he spotted the men following him. They were some distance behind him, maybe 200 metres.

The ground beneath Vikram's feet was uneven and he had to keep his head down to see where he placed his feet. The field wall abruptly ended and the ground rose in the form of a rocky slope. Vikram pounded up the slope. There was a ridge not far ahead.

A gunshot echoed sharply.

Vikram heard something strike the ground with tremendous force. "Oh no!" he gasped. Akira was resorting to firearms. Vikram did not stop. Drawing desperately on his energy resources, he pumped his legs faster. A second gunshot exploded and he heard the bullet slap into the mountain above his head. It threw dirt and pebbles at his face. It was only ten metres to the ridge. He would be safe on its other side as the mountainside would protect him. Vikram scrambled up the hill slipping on its loose soil. He used his hands, pulling himself upwards. His head had cleared the ridge when he heard the next gunshot. This time there was no ricochet. Vikram was sure that the bullet had hit him. There was no pain now but it would come later. He dived over the ridge and fell to the protected side of the mountain.

It was only when he rose to his feet that Vikram realised that the bullet had not struck him. There had been no ricochet because the bullet had shot past over the ridge. Except for bruised hands and knees he had not suffered any damage at all. Now an impenetrable mountain stood between him and Akira's gun. He was safe for the moment. He had breathing space. There was time to survey the mountains and choose his direction of flight. The ridge he had scrambled over was many kilometres in length. He had crossed its lower spur. The upper section rose skywards reaching for the summits above. Ahead the ground fell away and then rose again, sloping towards a similar parallel ridge which also stretched massively upwards.

There was no confusion in Vikram's mind about his objective. He had to steer his pursuers away from Rumbak. He would run from ridge to ridge, he decided, leading them on a wild-goose chase. Vikram ran towards the next ridge. Though the slope he sprinted across was gradual, he slipped, slid and tumbled down its crumbling surface.

There was a shout behind him. Two men had crested the previous ridge. There was no cover on the slope and he had been instantly spotted. Vikram kept running. The mountainside seemed endless, descending gradually, over several kilometres. Vikram halted suddenly. Losing altitude was foolish. It wasn't wise to have his pursuers above him as they would be able to track his every move. The situation would be reversed if he ran upwards. They would be below him and he would be able to keep an eye on their movements.

Vikram swung right. He was still running downhill but now he was heading towards the peaks instead of the valley. There were several men behind him now. The darkness prevented him from determining their exact number. There were more than two shadows, maybe four or five.

The slope soon ended and the climb to the next parallel

ridge began. Vikram's speed dropped to a gentle jog, but it quickly became apparent that he couldn't maintain this lesser gait either. There wasn't enough oxygen in the high-mountain air to sustain a rapid climb. Vikram gulped deeply and his lungs heaved. Though he pushed himself to the limit, he found it impossible to run. His calves hurt, his thighs ached and his lungs screamed at him, crying out that they were ready to burst. Vikram climbed on hands and knees. The use of his hands lessened the burden on his legs. Clutching rocks and gravel he pulled himself upwards. Forcing his protesting legs, he dragged them behind him. Akira's men closed in. The distance between Vikram and the men decreased dramatically. But once they began to climb, their speed dropped too.

The ceaseless exertion overheated Vikram's body. He unzipped his jacket. He yanked off his headgear and his gloves and stuffed them into his jacket pockets. Sweat soaked his clothes. It dripped on to his eyes obscuring his vision. Lowering his head he kept going. His pace was slow but it was steady.

The ridge he stumbled on to was wide and reasonably flat. Its far side slid away to another valley and then rose to another parallel ridge. However, this time Vikram did not descend. He was going to remain on this ridge. He decided that he would follow its wide stony surface up towards the mountains. Vikram could see the ridge rising gradually. Its distant end was lost in the shadows.

Vikram had successfully managed to divert his pursuers' attention. Now his only desire was to keep out of their clutches. Climbing high into the mountains was his best hope.

The moon slid behind a cloud and shadows swallowed Vikram as he ran. His pursuers were not always visible but the still night clearly carried the sound of their movements. Tiny clouds were flitting across the sky playing hide-and-seek with the moon. There was no wind. The extreme cold of the night no longer bothered him. Instead, the excess heat his body generated worried him. He had stripped off his jacket and wrapped it around his waist. He was tempted to remove his sweater as well, but he refrained from doing so. Running in nothing but a T-shirt, in near-freezing temperatures, was not sensible.

Vikram could feel himself beginning to tire. The day had been a long and strenuous one. He had climbed all the way to the snowline and then descended to the Rumbak valley. Now he was climbing again, at a speed his body could not sustain. He was thirsty too. The continuous sweating had drained moisture from his body. His mind was in a daze. Something warned him that his thought processes were not functioning smoothly. The lack of oxygen and his extreme exertion were affecting him. Every one of his little grey cells was occupied with the task of keeping his body moving. His will-power and resolve were being strained to their limits.

The pace of Vikram's pursuers was relentless. At the start they had been running a little more than 200 metres behind. The gap had widened initially, but then it had steadily begun to narrow. Now the frontrunners were just 100 metres behind — barely two minutes separated Vikram from them.

Rumbak was no longer visible. The ridge he had chosen was leading him high into the mountains. But now it was narrowing and up ahead it ended against a sheer mountainside. Vikram, who was climbing blindly, did not have a clue that his path would soon terminate. It was only when he was confronted by a vertical wall that he realised that his way forward was blocked.

Vikram looked around him in panic. The ridge had narrowed to just a few metres. His pounding heart missed a beat when he saw precipitous vertical drops on either side of him. Directly ahead was an unscaleable mountain wall. One of its walls curved, arching to the right. Vikram's eyes probed the curved section of the wall. Was there a path along its sheer surface? No, thought Vikram, there wasn't. What he was looking at could not be classified as a path. He was not a mountain goat.

Vikram flopped against the cliff. Strength had long vanished from the muscles in his legs and thighs. His limbs could barely support him. They were crumbling, dissolving in his sweat. His chest heaved uncontrollably and his lips were pushed permanently apart as he sucked at the thin mountain air. The kidnappers were no longer in a hurry. The pair in front had halted and were waiting for the others to catch up. Vikram's head sank; there was no escape for him.

It was some time before the men who had lagged behind caught up with the two in front. Vikram's breathing eased during that period and he discovered a welcome ability to focus his thoughts. There was no question of escape either to the right or to the left. His only hope was the sheer cliff that curved forward in the form of a hanging wall. The wall was not too wide, maybe about 30 metres across. He would be safe if he could somehow get across because, beyond it, the path which had so abruptly terminated, continued. He could push forward on the path ahead, resuming his climb. But that would be possible only if he could get across.

Vikram turned. The kidnappers numbered five in all. The stragglers had regained their breath and were moving forward. They walked slowly. There was no need to hurry, their quarry was trapped.

Vikram examined the wall. His eyes explored the possible path he had seen earlier. It wasn't something that could be called a track. Blue sheep or argali might have trotted across without blinking, but Vikram was not a mountain ungulate. Not exactly vertical the wall sloped at an extremely steep angle. One wrong step would result in a fall. The wall terminated in a ledge some 30 metres below. Anyone who stumbled or slipped would fall to that ledge.

Vikram looked at the kidnappers. Scarcely 30 seconds

of freedom remained. Someone had cracked a joke because Vikram heard them all break into laughter. The path, if he could call it one, was barely six inches wide and along many sections it did not exist. To negotiate these sections he would have to cling to the wall. Vikram scanned the wall for handholds.

The kidnappers were taunting him. They were challenging him to attempt the wall. Vikram never recalled what prompted him to step forward, but step forward he did. Striding to the edge of the path he swung his left foot onto the cliff wall, digging deep to secure a foothold. Holding the wall with his hands he brought his right foot across and placed it beside the left one.

The kidnappers barked incredulous yells. Vikram paid no heed to them. His right hand reached out grasping the next section of the wall. Assured that he had a firm grip he moved his right leg forward placing it securely on a narrow, clinging shelf. Like a crab Vikram edged forward, traversing the cliff wall. He did not dare look up or down. Handholds and footholds were all that mattered. If he continued to find secure ones, he could work his way across.

Vikram was surprised at himself. He was never comfortable with heights. The many knife-edged paths they had traversed during this trip had terrified him. With shaking feet and with a prayer on his lips, he had forced himself along those paths. But never had he dreamt of attempting a cliff like this.

The kidnappers had halted at the ridge edge. They silently watched Vikram thread his way across. One of them stepped onto the wall when Vikram neared the halfway point. The man moved fast, sliding across the wall like a monkey. He had obviously performed cliff traverses like this often. He searched out holds far quicker than Vikram. The kidnapper rapidly narrowed the distance between them.

Vikram found himself forced to move faster. He no longer had time to test each hold. If he had not been pushed Vikram

might have safely completed the crossing. But the looming presence of the mountain-savvy kidnapper hurried Vikram into choosing a hold he should not have. His hand gripped a protruding rock. Vikram usually tested each handhold by pulling hard on it before committing himself. If the hold held firm he would transfer his entire weight on to it and swing his legs forward. This time however, Vikram swung forward without testing his hold.

The rock crumbled under Vikram's weight and he felt himself slipping. Stones cascaded about him as he grabbed desperately for a handhold. But it was to no avail. He slid down the slope at a frightening speed. With gathering momentum his body plummeted down the rock surface. A spindly shrub, that he somehow managed to grab, broke his fall momentarily, but it could not hold him. It snapped loose from the mountain wall and Vikram felt himself falling.

The Amazing Dream

Caroline and Tsering had been safely hidden in the fields when the ledge collapsed beneath Vikram and Tashi. They had watched in horror as their friends tumbled to the ground.

"Where is he going?" cried Caroline when she saw Vikram running the wrong way. Then she realised that he was leading the kidnappers away.

"Come on Tsering," urged Caroline.

Choosing a direction opposite Vikram's they crawled on their hands and knees. They stayed close to the field wall and took care to see that neither of their heads cleared it. They cringed when they heard the sound of gunfire and looked back. Akira was standing on the terrace holding a handgun. Caroline clasped her mouth in horror as she watched Akira fire again and then again.

"Good boy, Vikram!" exclaimed Tsering when Vikram dived across the ridge.

Caroline too breathed a heartfelt sigh of relief. Vikram was safe. What about Tashi, where was he? The moon lit up the fields and the area outside Dorje's house. At first she did not see the little boy but later she noticed movements close to a row of large chortens. It could only be Tashi! Caroline saw him crawl behind one of the big dome-shaped structures. Tashi had crept away unnoticed while everybody's attention was focused on Vikram.

The fact that nobody had seen them enter the fields did not fool Caroline. Their safety could not be taken for granted. It might prove to be momentary. The kidnappers would soon discover that Vikram was on his own and that Tsering was not with him. Several men had run behind Vikram but one of them had halted. He was standing on the ridge that Vikram had dived across, with a pair of binoculars pressed to his eyes. This man could see the truth. At this very moment, he could possibly be concluding that Vikram was leading them on a futile chase.

The man would soon convey his observation to Akira. Their next move would be to comb the area for Tsering. Caroline was sure that they would search the fields. Dorje's house was too close for comfort. She had to find a safer place. There was a house at the far end of the field. They could hide behind it or even seek shelter inside it. There was no time to waste. Signalling Tsering to follow her, she crawled forward through the barley.

Akira was in a terrible rage. The lama had been stolen from him again. The kinship and admiration he had professed for Vikram vanished in an instant. When he saw Vikram dashing through the fields he had fired with the intention of knocking the boy down. Vikram, however, was a moving target and the distance had been too far for accurate marksmanship. His shaking hands did not help, either. Fury quivered through every vein and muscle in his body.

His stupid men! There were ten of them and yet they had not managed to prevent a breakout. The fools had failed. He was going to thrash the sentries, pulverise them, flatten them to the ground. Akira clenched his fists. But even as he stood there shaking with rage, his rational, calmer self began to assert itself. This was not the time for outbursts. All was not lost yet, there was still time to get the boy back.

Akira dashed down the stairs to his room. Collecting his shoes and jacket, he quickly slipped them on.

"Sir!" blurted a short, thickset man as Akira stepped out

of his room.

"What is it?" snapped Akira.

"The boy is alone, sir. None of the others are with him. I searched the area with my binoculars. He is running on his own."

Akira halted in mid-step. That boy! Was he attempting another diversion? Akira ran up to the terrace again. Vikram and his friends had escaped from the terrace. Standing there, Akira tried to reconstruct what had happened.

"Sir, come here, sir," requested the short man, who had followed Akira. "They escaped from here – that ledge broke under the boy's weight and he fell to the ground. We all woke then. It was the noise of his falling which alerted us."

"Was the boy Vikram, alone? Did you see the others?

"The boy was on the other side of the wall and running, when we first saw him. I cannot be sure, but I think he was alone when he fell."

Akira stared at the ground, deep in thought. The crumbling ledge must have taken Vikram by surprise and wrecked his plans of a silent getaway. Could the boy have made an instantaneous decision to mislead them? Very likely, concluded Akira. In such a situation, when the game was up, a diversion was a sensible course of action. If this was the strategy the boy had adopted, then where were the others? They had to be somewhere near by – waiting for Vikram to join them.

Akira shouted, calling his men. Hearing his summons, those that had remained behind assembled on the terrace. Akira positioned them along each wall of the terrace and instructed them to keep a sharp lookout.

"They are hiding somewhere here," he apprised them. "Search the fields. Look carefully about you and we will find them."

Akira stood beside his men but instead of searching he bowed his head, thinking deeply. It was the fields which were the most obvious hiding place. Their stone walls and barley offered the best cover. The houses that stood amongst the fields were also possible hiding places. Akira gritted his teeth. He would find Tsering; he would search every inch of the valley till he found the boy.

"Behind the chortens!" shouted one of the kidnappers. "There is somebody there." The man ran down the stairs, his companions following. Akira strode eagerly to the side of the terrace that faced the chortens. He saw his men pluck something out of the shadows. It was the Ladakhi boy they had captured earlier.

"Is Tsering with him?" asked Akira.

"No sir," came the reply.

"Question the boy. Search the area," ordered Akira.

Hope was returning to Akira. He was sure now that Vikram's sprint was a desperate attempt to divert their attention. The three boys had been forced to split up. Two had been found. Maybe the Ladakhi boy would reveal Tsering's hiding place.

Akira stood on the terrace while his men questioned Tashi. He was looking distractedly at the fields when he saw a flicker of movement from the corner of his eye. Akira stood still. It was a field on the left side of the valley. Amidst the silent, unmoving stands of barley, a few stalks had quivered. The fields were silver-white as the moon shone down upon them. A couple of minutes passed before he spotted the movement again.

Akira ran down the stairs. He crossed the courtyard and raced towards the fields. Quickly covering the distance, he halted short of the area where he had first spotted the movement. The stalks shook again. Akira moved stealthily forward and paused beside the stone wall. When the stalks shook once more, Akira jumped. Placing his hands on the wall he swung himself over it. The barely discernible movements suddenly exploded into frenzied motion. Akira leapt again. This time he landed on a small boy. Akira was gentle with Tsering. The boy was a lama. Not once had he treated him with disrespect and he was not about to do so now. Tsering calmly accepted his fate. Realising that there was no escape for him he stood peaceably where he was, staring at the kidnapper through his large, soulful eyes.

Caroline sobbed silently in the field. All that could possibly have gone wrong had done so. Her freedom did not console her. What did it matter? It was Tsering they wanted and they had got him. Why not her? Why the little boy? What wretched luck!

While crawling forward through the barley Tsering and she had separated. She had moved ahead of the boy, and it was while she was sitting still, waiting for him, that Akira had pounced. The shock and surprise of the attack had been absolute. There was nothing Caroline could do except watch.

Akira had led Tsering away. The man had no clue of her presence. None of the kidnappers had any idea of her existence. They had accounted for all the three boys and as far as they were concerned their search was over.

"Yes," thought Caroline bitterly. "It was all over!" Tsering would be flown out tomorrow and that would be the end of it. Caroline cried for Tsering. She cried for Vikram too. He had tried so hard, yet all his efforts had come to naught.

Vikram! Where was he? There was nothing she could do for Tsering, but if Vikram was in trouble maybe she could help him. Caroline did not want to spend the rest of the night crying alone in the barley. She wanted company...she craved company.

Vikram had disappeared over the ridge to the left. Caroline decided to climb the same ridge. But it would be unwise to climb from where she was hiding. She would be spotted the moment she stepped on to the slope. Luckily the same ridge continued all the way back to the valley head. She could walk back to the point where they had entered the Rumbak valley and climb it from there. Nobody would see her at that end.

Several lights illuminated Dorje's house. There was nobody on the terrace and Caroline doubted whether anyone was keeping a watch. They had Tsering now and she presumed that they were all gathered around their precious catch. There was no need to trouble herself by creeping stealthily through the fields; she walked instead, maintaining a crouched stance. Presently, a curve in the valley blocked off Dorje's house and she straightened herself. She was passing by a flag-strewn house when someone called. Caroline jumped when she heard her name being whispered.

Lobsang!

She had completely forgotten about him. Caroline embraced the boy when he came running to her. Lobsang's English was limited to a handful of words and there was little Caroline could communicate to him. Lobsang had witnessed all that had happened. He was aware of Tsering's recapture and in sign language he informed her of Tashi's capture too. Though distressed at learning of Tashi's fate, Caroline did not let her mind linger on it.

"Vikram?" she asked.

Lobsang nodded his head vigourously and pointed to the ridge above them.

"Yes, I know Vikram has gone there," said Caroline. She pointed to the ridge and repeated, "Vikram." Then she pointed to herself indicating that she was going to search for the boy.

Lobsang understood. "I come," he said. "Me come. You... me...Vikram."

Caroline smiled and hugged the boy. She had a companion now. Together they would find Vikram.

Vikram was dreaming. He had to be dreaming. There was an animal in front of him. It was standing above him.

Vikram found it extremely odd – he was below and the animal above. Could it be that he was lying on the ground? After considerable deliberation Vikram concluded that he was. He could not understand why he was sprawled there and that too at such an awkward angle.

The animal above him appeared silvery. It was a silver shadow against a backdrop of glittering stars. It had wonderful fluffy fur. Vikram couldn't help admiring its magnificent coat. The animal wasn't very tall and it had a long tail, almost as long as itself. The tail was silvery too. Two ears protruded from its head and he saw delicate whiskers on its snout. Its eyes glimmered in the faint moonlight and they were staring at him. Vikram gazed back at the eyes.

Now Vikram was convinced that he was dreaming. This gorgeous animal which stood above him was a snow leopard. "It isn't possible," thought Vikram. Only Raghu could find these mysterious ghosts of the Himalaya. This had to be a dream.

What a wonderful turn his dream had taken, but he remembered that it had had a frightening beginning. He could recall terrifying images of himself falling off a mountain. One image was particularly vivid – that of himself clutching at a mountain shrub which snapped under his weight and then the feeling of air whipping past his face. Such a fall would have had fatal consequences. Since Vikram was certain that he was alive the fall had to be part of a dream. The presence of the snow leopard confirmed that. Only in his dreams would he ever find a snow leopard.

The leopard stood motionless above him. Vikram decided that he could play the same game. If the animal wouldn't move, he wouldn't either. He wouldn't even blink.

The leopard wasn't a very large animal. For a carnivorous cat its face was rather small, much smaller than that of a tiger. Vikram chided himself at making such a stupid comparison; all leopards were smaller than tigers. Even little children knew that. But the leopard was infinitely more beautiful. Vikram had never seen such perfection in form: the handsome face; the glimmering eyes; the powerful shoulders; its thick furry paws and above all its glorious, radiant coat.

The animal moved. It settled itself on the slope below Vikram. It sat on its belly with legs outstretched. The animal held its head high, staring steadfastly at Vikram. Vikram saw the leopard's rosettes. The moon highlighted the dark splotches on the animal's resplendent fur.

What a wonderful dream...what an incredible dream. Vikram was happy, he could not have asked for more. Presently, a haze surrounded the leopard and his mind began to drift. He was losing the animal but it didn't matter, he was satisfied. He had had an eyeful of leopard.

Sometime later he opened his eyes again. The snow leopard had gone. All he could see were stars. Funny, the stars were below and the mountains above. It was odd indeed, but Vikram did not trouble himself too much about it. He wondered whether the snow leopard would return to his dream. There was a torch in his jacket pocket; if the animal returned he could shine his torch on it to see it better. Vikram tried to move his hand but experienced unexpected difficulty. It wasn't responding the way it should. Very often in dreams his limbs did not respond. Vikram decided to work hard at it. He would persevere till he had the torch. He was pleased with himself when his fingers finally encircled its thin metallic body. It took Vikram a considerable amount of time but he managed to extricate the torch from his pocket. Resting, he looked at the sky below. There were clouds in the great emptiness and they were playing games with the moon. Vikram saw rainbows circling the moon. "Rainbows around the moon?" Vikram laughed. Of course it wasn't possible – but how beautiful they looked. Vikram's mind started to drift once more and the stars dissolved into nothingness.

Sometime later the darkness resolved and the dream clicked on again. The leopard was back. It was sitting in front of him once more, but now beside it were two tiny animals. The little animals were replicas of their mother, identical in every respect, except that they were smaller — much smaller. Cute and cuddly are words that are not often associated with carnivorous cats, but these were the adjectives that sprang to Vikram's mind. The animals were balls of smoky fur, exquisite and delightful. Unlike their mother who sat statue-like, the little ones pranced about. They twitched their noses, yelped and directed immature, warbling growls at him. Vikram laughed. He couldn't help laughing at their belligerence.

But something strange happened when he laughed. The cubs suddenly backed away, leaping behind their mother. The mother crouched and stared at Vikram. Vikram looked back into her eyes. The moon went behind a cloud and the shimmering outlines of the animals turned to shadow. His torch; Vikram clicked it on. With a startled growl, the mother sprang back. The cubs scampered behind her. The animals were gone, even before he could blink.

Vikram tried unsuccessfully to turn his head. "Come back!" he heard himself shout. But all Vikram saw was the stars, and soon they too flickered and faded.

A Wish Fulfilled

Lobsang found a fold in the valley that shielded them from Dorje's house. It was a safe spot from which to climb the ridge. Lobsang guided Caroline upwards and she plodded behind him, sweating profusely. After a long, seemingly endless climb, they topped out on the ridge. The valley which Vikram had run to was visible below. Lobsang led Caroline to where the mountain sloped down again. Finding a heap of boulders that screened them from Rumbak, they settled themselves.

Lobsang touched Caroline's shoulder and pointed. Four shadows were about to descend into the Rumbak valley. The shadows were on the same ridge they stood on but much lower down, directly above the fields. They could only be the men who had run behind Vikram. Caroline flattened herself against the mountainside and so did Lobsang.

She reached into her jacket pocket for her binoculars. Pressing them to her eyes she focussed them on the kidnappers. "Thank God," she breathed when she did not spot Vikram's familiar outline.

Lobsang confirmed what Caroline saw. "No Vikram," he said, even though he did not have binoculars.

The men were returning from a fruitless search. Caroline spotted one more shadow, well behind the first four. Caroline was puzzled with his appearance at first. But she quickly concluded that he was part of the same team – a straggler who had fallen behind. The man was descending the ridge ahead and his position provided Caroline with a bearing on the direction Vikram had taken. Vikram must have climbed the ridge the man was descending. He could be somewhere on it, or beyond it. As Caroline peered at the darkness she began to comprehend the scale of the search she planned to undertake. All she could see was shadows. Darkness blanketed the hundreds of square kilometres of mountain that lay spread before her. Vikram was but a speck in the vastness and the very thought of spotting him seemed ridiculous.

Caroline watched the kidnappers. As long as they moved they were visible; if they halted they merged with the darkness. Visibility was *that* poor. Her only hope was to search for movement. Caroline decided that she would try. No matter how impossible the task seemed, she was going to attempt it. Despite the odds she would find Vikram. She had to!

Clouds hampered the moon as Caroline probed the darkness with her binoculars. The mountains were alternately flooded with its pale light and swamped by gloom. Little Lobsang searched the mountains too. The Ladakhi boy had grown up amidst them and the chances were that if Vikram was to be found, it would be he who would find him.

Caroline concentrated on trying to trace the path Vikram might have taken. She started with the slope where she had spotted the straggler. The slope led to a ridge. The outlines of the ridge were clearly visible but beyond it lay deep shadow. The darkness beyond was absolute; if Vikram had gone there, even Lobsang would be unable spot him. Caroline narrowed the scope of her search to the ridge. It was a massive ridge that stuck out from the foot of the mountain like the root of a tree. The ridge was the root and the solid, rising mountain, the trunk. Caroline followed the ridge to where it disappeared into the mountain. The mountain rose perpendicularly from where the ridge met it. The size of the mountains here never failed to stagger Caroline. Though the ridge climbed a fair distance, eighty percent of the mountain still towered above the point where the ridge fused with it.

Caroline's eyes explored the section of the mountain where the ridge merged with it. This was the only area worth searching, she concluded. The section of mountain was visible and within range of her binoculars.

Caroline searched so hard that her eyes began to hurt. All she saw was shadow and deeper shadow. Yet the girl persisted. She lost track of time as she scanned featureless rock, sharp slopes and boulder piles. Every five minutes or so, when double images began to disorient her, she would hand over the binoculars to Lobsang. She rested her eyes during these intervals, gently massaging them with the palms of her hands. It was a half-hour later that Caroline's diligence was rewarded.

She was scanning a level, moonlit section of mountain when she sucked in her breath. Had a shadow moved on the rubble-strewn slope? Caroline slowly swung her binoculars back, retracing their traverse across the slope. What had she seen? She carefully surveyed the faintly illumined slope, searching for a flicker of shadow. Caroline focussed her undivided attention on the mountain. She saw the blur again.

No! It could not be!

"Oh my God!" exclaimed Caroline aloud. "Oh God... daddy. Dad, have I found snow leopards?"

Caroline cast away her doubts as her eyes fastened onto a flickering discontinuity. The fuzzy image sharpened as she gazed at it. Three silver shadows were visible, one large and two small. What Caroline was gazing disbelievingly at was a snow leopard family.

Caroline's eyes filled with tears. "Daddy...dad, I can see snow leopards. Dad, can you see what I am seeing?" Her voice shook as she talked to her long-dead father. "This is amazing. There are three of them dad, it's a family... like Lara, Zara and their mom. These snow leopards are wild and free, not like ones we would see at the zoo. Dad, they look like silver ghosts."

Yes, the animals were ghosts. They were so indistinct, so indefinite, that she wondered how she had picked out their shadows. Caroline was convinced that it was divine intervention that had enabled her to spot the animals. It was her father who had led her to them. Caroline's hands were shaking. But she somehow managed to control them, trapping the animals in her field of vision.

Caroline was overcome with emotion. The image of her father swam before her eyes. She had despaired of ever seeing his beloved snow leopards. She had resigned herself to returning home without fulfilling her father's dream. But now on this frozen mountain, under the pale radiance of the moon, her wish had come true. She would cherish this wondrous vision and it would remain with her forever.

Lobsang spotted the animals the moment Caroline pointed them out to him. He picked out their silvery profiles with bare eyes. The leopards walked in single file, the cubs following in the tracks of their mother. "Exactly as Raghu had said," recalled Caroline as she tracked them with her binoculars.

The search for Vikram was put on hold as they followed the movements of the snow leopard family. The animals were walking beneath a huge, dark cliff. After a short walk, they halted abruptly. Raghu had said that at moments like these, when a snow leopard freezes, it vanishes into the mountain.

Caroline's fingers pressed tightly into the casing of her lenses. She had lost the family. All she could see was pale, formless rock. It was the cubs that enabled Caroline to locate the animals again. Two tiny blurs betrayed the presence of the family. The blurs became extremely active as the little animals pranced about. After a couple of minutes Caroline began to wonder whether there was something on the ground beside them. The cubs displayed a keen interest in a nearby shadow, leaping towards it and then backing off. Caroline was intrigued by the shadow. It wasn't a rock nor was it some mountain formation; there was something strange and unusual about it. She wondered what it could be.

Could it be prey? Was that why the cubs were giving it their undivided attention? It wasn't live prey; the lack of movement ruled that out. Could it be the carcass of a kill? Maybe the family was returning to feed on a carcass.

A cloud swept across the moon.

"Darn," muttered Caroline as she lost the animals once again.

Suddenly, like a glowing needle, a ray of light stabbed the darkness. Moonlight returned and Caroline, whose attention was concentrated on the animals, spotted them again. The cubs seemed frozen to the ground, then breaking into motion, they backed away. Their mother appeared to retreat too. The beam of light was stationary for a few seconds and then it began to move. It rolled and then it began to bounce. There were three bounces before it finally halted.

"Flashlight?" thought Caroline, not sure of herself.

"Torch!" shouted Lobsang excitedly.

"Torch?" Caroline remembered that in this country 'flashlights' were called 'torches'. The light was undoubtedly the beam of a flashlight. But where had the flashlight come from? "Never mind," thought Caroline as she searched for the snow leopards again. They were walking hurriedly back, along the way they had come. The flashlight had obviously scared them away.

"Vikram!" cried Lobsang.

Absorbed with the snow leopards, Caroline wondered why Lobsang was talking of Vikram.

"Binocular," requested Lobsang urgently.

"Why?" asked Caroline unwillingly. "I am watching the snow leopards."

"Pliss...Vikram!"

The girl reluctantly handed them over wondering where Lobsang might have spotted Vikram. Lobsang glued the lenses to his eyes. The shadow! Was that what Lobsang was thinking about? The flashlight! Could it be Vikram's flashlight? Caroline stared at the Ladakhi boy.

Lobsang remained silent, gazing through the binoculars for a long time.

Caroline bit her lip.

"Vikram there," he said finally.

Caroline snatched the binoculars from him and pressed them to her eyes. She located the mysterious shadow that the cubs had stood beside. Caroline froze. Were her eyes playing tricks on her or had the shadow moved? There was a deathly stillness within Caroline. Was that shadow a human being? If it was, then something was the matter with it. The movement she had seen was like a feeble shiver. Then the shadow had turned still again. Why was it not reaching out to the fallen flashlight? There was something amiss. If that was Vikram then he was obviously hurt.

"Vikram fall...hurt, we go!"

Lobsang had already risen to his feet. Caroline scrambled after the Ladakhi boy. She followed Lobsang blindly, slipping and stumbling after him. Her mind was numb. Had Vikram fallen down the mountain? She wanted that shadow to be Vikram and yet she didn't want it to be him. She prayed as she ran, appealing to the Almighty for the wellbeing of her friend.

Their destination was clearly marked by the stationary beam of the flashlight. Lobsang set a cracking pace. He led her across scree slopes, along ridges, over boulders and through endless sections of desolate mountain. Caroline was amazed at her ability to keep up with him. She was drained, both physically and emotionally. Her body was tapping a hidden source of energy. The mysterious energy propelled her forward, pumping her lungs and driving her legs.

Caroline looked often at the torch hoping that their journey would end soon. Its pinprick of light remained constant, never getting larger or smaller. About half an hour into their march it disappeared behind a mountain. Its location was evidently imprinted in Lobsang's mind because thereafter they did not see its guiding light for a long time. When it finally reappeared, its beam was much closer and directly ahead of them. Caroline knew they were almost there and when she spotted the shadow, she sprinted the final distance, overtaking Lobsang.

The Plan

Vikram was lying at the bottom of a cliff-like slope. Caroline choked back a sob as she ran. The towering slope told the story. Vikram had fallen down the mountain. Caroline threw herself beside her friend's supine body. There was blood on his face and his eyes were shut. Cradling his head in her hands Caroline repeated Vikram's name over and over again.

Vikram lay silent and still.

Tears streamed down Caroline's cheeks as she reached into her rucksack and pulled out her water-bottle. Lobsang took it from her shaking hands. Caroline stroked Vikram's hair while Lobsang uncorked the bottle. There were long gashes on Vikram's cheeks and his face was caked with blood and dirt. Lobsang gently dripped water on Vikram's forehead.

Caroline felt movement beneath her fingers.

Vikram opened his eyes. He stared unseeingly at the sky before closing them again. With wet fingers Caroline carefully cleaned his eyes, brushing away the grit and dust. Vikram's mouth was open and Lobsang slowly trickled water into it.

Vikram was lying at an extremely odd angle, with his legs above — on the rising section of the slope — and his head below. Motioning Lobsang to help, they gently lifted him. Despite Vikram's silence Caroline sensed his agony. He gritted his teeth and his fingers clamped tightly around Caroline's wrists. Finding a level area, they gently laid him down.

Vikram did not speak for several minutes. His eyes remained shut and he lay unmoving. Caroline reached for his hands and pulled back in horror. Vikram's hands were bloodied, scarred and bruised. Caroline shuddered and instinctively looked up at the slope above. Was it the lacerated hands that had saved his life? He must have clung on to rocks and bushes as he fell. Vikram's external injuries were visible. But what about internal ones? He could not have survived such a fall without breaking some bones. Caroline decided to treat the injuries that she could. There was disinfectant and cotton in her backpack. Laying her tiny medical kit on the ground, she set about cleaning Vikram's wounds.

Vikram kept his eyes shut.

"I dreamt I saw a snow leopard," he said presently. His voice was hoarse and his eyes remained shut.

Caroline paused from her work but she did not speak.

"I saw its cubs too."

There was a long interval before Vikram spoke again. Caroline allowed him to talk, not saying a word.

Vikram described his dream. He spoke first about the terrible nightmare of falling off a mountain. The memory was so amazingly real that he was not sure whether it was a dream or had actually happened. But that kind of a fall would have resulted in instant death. The fact that he was alive proved that it was a dream. After the fall his dream had steadily improved. Vikram described his fascinating tryst with the snow leopard family. He wished this part of the dream was true because he could never have hoped for such a splendid encounter with the animals. The leopards had come so close to him. They were so life-like, so real and so beautiful. It was a thrilling vision and he wished it could have gone on, but it had ended abruptly when, during the dream, he had flashed a torch.

Caroline rose and fetched Vikram's fallen torch.

"It wasn't a dream, Vikram," she said holding the torch

above his face. "The snow leopards were real, we saw them too. Your flashlight scared them away. Lobsang and I saw everything. We saw you drop the flashlight and we came running. Everything you remember is true, Vikram. Nothing was a dream, not even your falling off the mountain. You have taken a horrid fall and you are lucky to be alive."

Vikram was silent. Caroline continued to work on him, squeezing disinfectant and cleaning his wounds.

"Where's Tsering?" asked Vikram presently.

"Can you try sitting up?" requested Caroline, quickly changing the topic. "I need to assess the damage to your bones."

They raised Vikram to a sitting position. Caroline supported him, with an arm around his shoulders. Lobsang fed Vikram the remaining water and he gratefully gulped it down.

"I get," said Lobsang taking the empty bottle from Vikram. There was a fresh-water stream nearby. He smiled reassuringly at Vikram and disappeared into the darkness.

Refreshed by the water, Vikram asked Caroline to help him rise to his feet. Like Caroline he was anxious to know the extent of his injuries.

Caroline held his waist and Vikram placed his arms around her. Caroline rose slowly. Vikram leaned heavily on her as she lifted him off the ground.

"Test each leg," instructed Caroline.

Vikram's left leg could hold his weight, but he winced when his right leg touched the ground. Caroline then slowly lowered him, laying him flat once more. She proceeded to gently prod his arms, shoulders, legs, chest and neck. Vikram flinched twice. First when she pressed his chest and once more when she touched his left shoulder.

"Your guardian angel is taking good care of you," smiled Caroline after her inspection. "When I first saw you – the way your body was lying – I thought you were dead. You got away lightly, Vikram dear. Only your leg, chest and shoulder; two broken bones and maybe a cracked rib. That's nothing for the kind of fall you took."

Lobsang returned with a large smile and a bottle filled with cold mountain water.

"Where is Tsering?" repeated Vikram after consuming more than half the bottle.

Caroline did not avoid the question this time and she somberly related the night's events.

There was no change in Vikram's expression, but Caroline, whose arm still supported him, felt his shoulders sag.

"Akira is not going to get away," said Vikram when Caroline finished. There was quiet conviction in his voice. "We are going to rescue Tsering."

Caroline refrained from passing any comment. Vikram's desire was noble but any rescue was impossible. He couldn't even walk, with a broken bone in his leg.

Vikram lapsed into deep thought. During that period Caroline washed his face and finished off the last of her disinfectant. Finally Vikram spoke. "There is a way," he said. "We can do it." Caroline was skeptical to begin with, but as Vikram spoke she turned hopeful. Vikram talked at length and when he concluded Caroline acknowledged that there could be an outside chance. Even though the probability of success was low they both agreed that an attempt had to be made.

The plan involved abandoning Vikram. The broken bone in his leg ruled out any role for him in this final rescue effort. He would have to wait here till a stretcher was organised to carry him back to Rumbak. The stretcher, Caroline informed him, would also be required later to carry him all the way to Leh.

Caroline had biscuits in her backpack and she left them behind for Vikram along with her bottle which Lobsang obligingly filled once more. It was already late. There was no time to waste. Caroline hugged Vikram gently, careful not to hurt his damaged ribs and kissed him goodbye.

"Our plan is going to work," said Vikram in farewell. "It will!"

"Of course it will," smiled Caroline. "You look after yourself and don't worry your head about it. Tsering will be waiting to greet you when you return to Rumbak."

Vikram watched them depart. The sky was still dark but dawn was not far away. The helicopter was scheduled to arrive at eight. Caroline had three hours.

Aditya looked at his watch. It was almost five. It was Aditya's uneasiness that had woken him. He lay in his sleeping bag, drowsily wondering why he was so anxious.

Tsewang!

The camp boy was supposed to have woken him as soon as he returned. He had promised Aditya that he would stop by and inform him about Vikram's camp. But Tsewang had not.

Aditya sat up in his sleeping bag.

Why hadn't Tsewang come? Distinctly uneasy now, Aditya decided to investigate. He slipped on his gloves, tucked on his woollen headgear and wrapped a thick scarf around his neck. He zipped his jacket and torch in hand, stepped out of his tent. Despite his elaborate preparations for the cold, Aditya shivered and hunched his shoulders as he hurried towards Tsewang's tent.

"Tsewang," he whispered, halting beside the tent.

There was no answer.

Bending, Aditya unzipped the flaps and repeated his call.

Aditya flicked on his torch. The tent was empty, Tsewang's sleeping bag had not been slept in.

Tsewang had not returned! He had promised to be back in two hours and seven had passed. Aditya's worry multiplied several fold. While he stood outside the tent wondering what to do, he was disturbed by the sound of footsteps.

"Good morning, Aditya." It was Raghu. "Nice to see you

up so early." Raghu had his boots on. The morning twilight revealed that he was fully dressed.

"I thought I heard wolves howling," explained Raghu. "So, an hour ago, I went to look for them but I didn't see any. What are you doing up so early?"

Aditya unburdened his fears to the wildlife researcher.

"Yes, Tsewang's absence worries me," said Raghu thoughtfully after Aditya had spoken. "But I am not sure what the disappearance of the Swedes' cook has got to do with the whole affair. Tsewang is a conscientious boy and should have come back by now. It is already past his wake up time; he starts his chores by five. It was wrong to send him without taking my permission, Aditya. His absence is going to disrupt the running of the camp. Don't ever do that again."

Aditya mumbled an apology to Raghu. He offered to go to the other camp and bring Tsewang back. "I asked him to go," said Aditya penitently. "It's my responsibility to see that he returns safely."

"I'll come with you," said Raghu. "It's too late for sleep now. Go and get dressed."

Aditya dressed hurriedly, pulling on several layers of warm clothes. He walked back to the kitchen tent where Raghu waited for him. Glimmers were spreading in the eastern sky when they set off.

Raghu led the way. Like Tsewang, he knew the shortcut between the camps.

"Partridge," informed Raghu, when they heard loud clucking from the mountainside.

The glow in the east spread across the sky. Birds announced the arrival of a new day. It was a crisp, cold morning beneath a cloudless sky. Raghu helpfully explained every birdcall they heard. Redstarts, snowcocks, wagtails, choughs...Rahgu did not have to see them; he identified them by their calls.

There was an unending series of mountains on their left,

all deep in shadow. To their right, the higher snow-capped peaks glistened in the golden glow of the rising sun.

Both Raghu and Aditya halted when they heard a shout from the slopes above. A man in long woollen clothes was running down to meet them.

"Karma, our horseman," said Raghu as the man came in closer. "I wonder whether the wolves got any of his horses?"

As camp was to be shifted today, Karma had returned to round up his animals. His horses and donkeys were required to carry the heavy luggage. Three days earlier, when camp two had been established, Karma had set his animals free. It was his practice to allow his animals to roam the pastures and feed while there was no work. The horses, of course, preferred the higher regions where the pastures were greener. This inclination of theirs increased Karma's legwork tremendously. The poor man always had his work cut out for him on a camp shifting day.

"Did the wolves get any of your horses?" asked Raghu when the horseman arrived.

Karma was lightly built and reedy thin. "Yes, those nasty animals did!" replied Karma angrily. "Luckily they did not manage to bring down the horse they caught. They bit him in his leg, but he managed to fight them off." Karma paused to gather his breath. "It is not about my horses that I have come to you," he continued. "It's about what's been happening at the village. Gunshots were fired in Rumbak last night. There are bad men in the village. They arrived last evening with the boy Tsering from your camp..."

"No!" exclaimed Aditya in dismay.

"Yes, they have the boy with them. Everybody in the village is upset. They didn't like these men to begin with and then came the shooting at night. It is troubling everybody. I met old Dorje on the way here. He had rented his house to the men for the night. He too is angry with them."

Aditya's fears had not been unfounded. Akira had struck!

Tsering was in their clutches. The kidnapper had raided Vikram's camp the previous evening. That was why there had been no response to the radio call, and why Tsewang had not returned.

Raghu saw and understood the shock in Aditya's eyes. "Camp one is visible from around the next bend," he told Aditya. "Follow me, we'll have a look."

Raghu and Aditya ran. After several minutes of hard running, when they topped a rise, Raghu cautioned Aditya. "Careful," he said. "Don't skyline yourself."

The camp was a collection of coloured smudges at the foot of a massive brown mountain. Two figures were seated awkwardly on the ground outside the tents. They pulled out their binoculars.

"Their hands are tied behind their backs!" exclaimed Aditya.

While they watched, three more figures emerged from the tent, all with their hands locked behind their backs. Two strange men appeared. Their hands were free and one of them had a gun buckled to his belt.

"Where's Vikram?" asked Aditya staring through his lenses.

"I don't see Caroline either," observed Raghu.

Wangchuk the cook and Yuan Lee, were seated separately. Tina and Kathy, along with Tsewang, sat opposite them. It was obvious that neither Vikram nor Caroline were in the group.

"Tashi is not there either," observed Raghu.

Aditya had lowered his binoculars. Karma had said that there had been gunfire at the village. Had Vikram attempted to free Tsering? Could Caroline and Tashi be with him? Maybe, thought Aditya. Could Vikram have been captured too? No, that couldn't be as Karma had only mentioned Tsering.

Raghu had lowered his binoculars and he was looking at Aditya.

"Those gunshots which Karma spoke of," said Aditya. "It might have been Vikram trying to rescue Tsering. Something must have taken place during the night. I'm going to Rumbak to find out."

"We'll go together," said Raghu.

Dawn broke as Caroline and Lobsang walked to Rumbak. Caroline intended to enter Rumbak through its usual entrance, at the mouth of the valley. She would pretend to be a backpacker. None of Akira's people, not even Akira himself, had set eyes on her. They were not even aware of her existence. Caroline looked like a typical foreign tourist and she intended to use her anonymity to her advantage.

After a long, hard walk they entered the river gorge and met the trekking trail that led to Rumbak. The river gurgled noisily amidst stands of juniper and poplar. Though the peaks of the mountains were bathed in sunlight, the gorge was in shadow. The morning chill was fresh and bracing.

After covering some distance along the trail they heard the soft tinkle of bells.

"Ponies," said Lobsang.

They spotted the animals round the next bend. A team of Ladakhi ponies was crossing the river.

"Run!" shouted Lobsang, suddenly charging forward.

Confused, Caroline ran behind the boy. She had no idea why he had suddenly dashed forward.

Lobsang sped towards the ponies and leapt onto one of them just as it was about to cross the river. The river was only 20 feet across but it was knee deep and its waters were freezing. By clinging on to the pony Lobsang crossed the river without wetting his feet. Caroline followed his example and a placid little pony carried her uncomplainingly across.

After an hour of steady walking they emerged from the shade of the gorge onto a sunlit plain. Caroline welcomed the warmth of the sun. Two colourfully dressed trekkers walked ahead of her. The large white tent at the mouth of the Rumbak valley was visible. A short walk brought them to its entrance.

Robbery At Rumbak

The sun lit up the white fabric of the tent creating a warm glow. The bustle and clutter inside sounded cheerful and friendly. Caroline breathed deeply. For the first time since the previous evening the tension within her eased, allowing her to relax. Her nostrils twitched at the smell of food. It was a delicious aroma and her eyes sought its source. She spotted a counter at the far end of the tent. Behind it stood a smiling young Ladakhi girl. A tiny baby was tied securely to her back. Clouds of steam billowed from a pot placed on a kerosene stove beside her. Stringy, white noodles were simmering in the pot. But the tent did not have much else to offer. Only noodles, biscuits and mint tea were available. Caroline ordered all three.

Plastic tables and chairs were scattered around the periphery of the tent. While Caroline seated herself, Lobsang slipped behind the counter. Next to the young Ladakhi lady sat an old man and Caroline saw Lobsang engage him in conversation. Caroline assumed that the man behind the counter was Dorje, the gentleman who had rented his house to Akira. Lobsang had informed her that Dorje was available at the cafeteria tent every morning. It was his granddaughter who owned and managed the tent. The old man's cooperation was vital for the success of Vikram's plan.

Lobsang talked earnestly to Dorje. After listening intently for a while, the old man turned to look at Caroline. He was really old, thought Caroline. His face was deeply wrinkled and when he smiled only two teeth were visible. Caroline returned the smile and bowed her head.

Dorje's granddaughter crossed to Caroline and placed a bowl of steaming noodles before her. The granddaughter was young, probably no older than Caroline herself – yet she had a baby. Caroline smiled her thanks and then shook her head in wonderment. Life moved at different speeds in villages and cities.

The smell of the noodle stew was intoxicating. Slipping off her jacket she attacked her breakfast voraciously. The noodles were hot and wholesome and she savoured and slurped each spoonful.

Caroline absorbed herself in her meal and only after the keen edge of her hunger had been satisfied did she begin to look about her. The table beside hers was occupied by a pair of teenagers, both wearing jackets she was familiar with. 'University Of Washington' was emblazoned in large letters on their clothing. The sweatshirt Caroline wore was stamped with the same logo.

"You from Seattle too?" enquired a boy who wore one of the jackets. His face was flushed and it was obvious that he was tired. He had not shaved for days and the signs of a patchy beard were visible. "Man," he continued after Caroline nodded, "I find it difficult to breathe here."

"What do you expect, Tim?" said the girl sitting beside him. "You're not back home in Seattle. We are at 14,000 feet. Halfway to the top of Mount Everest." Though the girl's features were Indian, she spoke with a perfect American accent. She had a rich, brown complexion and large, lively eyes.

"Don't," pleaded Tim, grimacing and holding out his hands. "Don't talk to me about Everest. I'm already choking here. God, it must be awful up there on the peaks and in the snow."

"It's not so bad," said Caroline, wiping her mouth with the back of her sleeve. "I was up there yesterday. We were above the snowline – maybe 18,000 feet. Breathing was

easy, except when you climbed. You have to go slow then, halt every once in a while and get your breath back."

"You were up there?" There was an incredulous expression on Tim's face.

"Yeah," said Caroline laughing. "It's no big deal. You can get there too. Just make sure that you are acclimatised properly." Caroline was happy to laugh and chat. But the conversation felt so unreal, especially at a moment like this, when she was about to embark on a dangerous venture.

Caroline glanced at Lobsang and Dorje. The two were still deep in conversation. Rising, she collected her noodle bowl and crossed to the table where the youngsters were seated. Talking to them would help keep her mind on pleasant things.

The girl's name was Radha. She introduced herself to Caroline as a resident of Seattle.

"This guy, Tim," smiled Radha, "is worried about everything. Just look at him."

Tim was staring suspiciously at the cup of mint tea that had been placed before him.

"You should see him with the water we drink. He's insanely distrustful about water. He has this special filter and all kinds of purifying tablets, even though our camp cook gives us boiled water. Go on Tim, put one of your tablets in your tea."

"The tea has been boiled," said Caroline assuringly. "You can drink it."

Tim grudgingly sipped from his cup.

"The water here flows down from the glaciers," said Caroline. "It can't get any purer than that."

"But what if some mountain goat has peed in it?"

"That's why they boil if for you," said Radha.

Lobsang and Dorje had risen to their feet. Caroline gulped down her remaining noodles and rose when they approached.

"*Jule*," said Dorje with a toothy smile.

"*Jule*," replied Caroline, folding her hands together.

Lobsang handed Caroline an old weather-beaten rucksack that he had collected from behind the counter. Caroline smiled and accepted it.

"Come," said Lobsang.

Caroline nodded. "Nice meeting you Tim, Radha," she said, bidding them goodbye.

"You off?"

"Just to the village. Should be back soon." Caroline smiled and waved as she walked out of the tent.

The rucksack that Lobsang had handed her was much larger than the little daypack strapped to her back. Halting outside the tent she transferred her little pack into the larger one.

"Those men bad," said Dorje, standing beside Caroline.

"Yes, very bad," replied Caroline. "You speak English?"

"Little," replied Dorje. The wrinkles on his face fused into thick folds as he smiled. "I learn in restaurant. Lobsang tell me what you want. I help. We all scared when they shoot last night. I no want their money. I want them to go."

"Has Lobsang told you what we plan to do?" asked Caroline.

"Yes. You no worry," Dorje assured her, smiling again. "I tell bad men that you stay in my house. You forget things in house. You need now...we go inside."

"Yes," smiled Caroline. "We go inside. Then I try." Caroline laughed and shrugged her shoulders.

Dorje laughed with her.

Caroline glanced at her watch. It was 7:15 a.m.

"Go?" asked Lobsang.

Caroline nodded.

A cheerful voice spoke up from behind Caroline. "Still here?" it questioned.

Caroline turned. It was Tim and with him was Radha. They had stepped out of the tent.

"I'm leaving now," smiled Caroline.

"Can we come with you?" asked Radha. "We have plenty of time before our camp mates arrive. We'd like to see the village."

Caroline hesitated, then shrugged. "Sure," she said. "You're welcome."

Lobsang did not accompany them. The kidnappers had seen him earlier when he took Vikram's note across to them. His presence could alert them. Caroline sped a flying kiss at him as they departed.

Radha chatted with Caroline as they followed Dorje. She explained she was a second generation Indian American. Her parents, both from Punjab, had immigrated to the States before she was born. She had visited India often but this was the first time without her parents. She and Tim were part of a large American trekking group, all from the same school in Seattle. The rest of the group would arrive at Rumbak later, around noon. The reason she and Tim had parted from their group was because all the others had volunteered to climb a small peak. Only Tim and she had declined and had walked on to Rumbak instead.

Caroline assessed Radha as she spoke. Both she and Tim seemed trustworthy. But she wondered whether they would help her if she asked them? She needed to somehow distract Akira and his men. Their presence could prove to be useful.

Caroline decided to make the request. "I need your help," she said. She paused and looked at Tim and Radha who were both gazing questioningly at her. "I know it's not correct, asking for help from people whom I hardly know, but I have no choice. I don't have the time to explain. There is something terrible going on in this village. A boy has been kidnapped and an terrible fate awaits him unless I do something about it. Only I can help him and for my plan to work I might need help."

"Wow!" said Tim.

"What kind of help?" asked Radha cautiously.

"Old man Dorje here is leading us to the house where the kidnappers have camped for the night. The leader of the kidnappers has a satellite phone in his possession. I need that phone to make a call. The call is important because a helicopter is coming here soon. I have to stop that helicopter. To do that I will have to steal the phone."

"Wow!" repeated Tim.

"Dorje is going to tell the kidnappers that I had stayed in his house a few days ago and that I had left behind some luggage. It is a ruse to let me in. Once I am inside I will need you to distract the main kidnapper. He is a Japanese man who speaks English. If you can talk to him and hold his attention...that's all I will need. I know where the phone is. I need less than a minute to put it in my pack."

"Will we get into trouble?" asked Tim worriedly. "I don't want to be jailed."

"There is no jail out here, Tim," said Radha.

"There aren't any police either," said Caroline. "If there were I wouldn't require your help."

"I'll help you," said Radha. "I don't understand what's going on, but I trust you."

"Thanks!" said Caroline sincerely. "I mean it."

"You'll have to take me out for dinner for this," said Tim. "I don't work for free."

"Done," smiled Caroline. "Dinner for you in Leh and back home in Seattle too."

Dorje, despite his age, had a sprightly step and he led them briskly forward. They passed the chortens. There were several large ones standing in a row like giant chess pieces. Daylight had turned the dark fields Caroline had hidden in, into colourful green oases. Dorje's house was visible ahead. There was considerable activity within its compound. Men were busily walking about and luggage was being piled at the door.

"Let's stay together," suggested Caroline. "Make us laugh, Tim. Crack some jokes. I want them to think that we are on a morning stroll."

The Rumbak stream sparkled as they stepped across it on conveniently placed stones. Dorje led them towards the main gate of the house. Opening it he smiled and invited them to follow.

Several men stood in the compound gazing at them. A short, squat Tibetan walked forward. Stepping in front of Dorje he barred the way.

A loud conversation ensued. The Americans did not understand a single word.

"My bag," interrupted Caroline with a bright smile. She gestured with her hands outlining a backpack. "I left it behind here and I need it because I am going to Leh today."

"*Hamara* backpack," said Radha in accented Hindi. "We want our bag."

"We have to get her bag," contributed Tim in an earnest tone. "It's important you know – she's going to take me out for dinner when we get back."

The combined volume of four voices was too much for the man to handle. Ordering Dorje to wait at the door, he backed away. Entering the house he mounted the steps to the first floor.

Tim was in a cheery mood and while they waited he wandered around the compound saying "*Jule*," to every man he came across. Some of the men smiled. Others muttered and turned away.

The squat man returned shortly and to Caroline's relief he invited them in. Dorje led them into the house and showed them the way to the stairs.

"Dorje, sir," said Tim at the top of the stairs. "You have a neat pad."

It was indeed a nice place. Sunlight poured in from the rectangular terrace opening above, lighting up the floor. Caroline, who had not had the time to appreciate the house earlier, took notice now.

"Just look at all the space, Radha," said Tim. "We could

have a party here."

The sitting room door was shut but the other doors were open. A strong smell of coffee came from the kitchen.

Tim twitched his nostrils. "Coffee...wow!"

Caroline wondered where Akira was. Only the sitting room doors were shut. Could he be there? Was Tsering there too?

The squat man said something to Dorje.

The old man turned to Caroline. "Look now," he said.

"Talk to the short guy," whispered Caroline as she turned away from her friends and walked to the open store-room door.

Tim sauntered over to the squat man. Halting before him he dug into his pocket and pulled out a large chocolate bar.

"Here, try this," he offered the man. "It's good American chocolate."

"Indian chocolate is better," said Radha, positioning herself between the man and the store-room.

The squat man looked at Tim and shook his head.

"Come on," persuaded Tim. "Don't listen to this lady. She's got it all wrong. She's confused, she cannot make up her mind whether she is Indian or American. This chocolate is the best in the world. Have some, you will like it. Mr. Dorje, sir, you have some too."

Dorje's wrinkled face crinkled as he smiled and accepted a piece.

Caroline entered the store-room. She unhitched the large backpack and unzipping it, pulled out her original daypack.

A smile had appeared on the squat man's face. Tim interpreted the amused expression as an indication of acceptance.

"Give me the bar," said Radha. "I'll unwrap it. Why don't you show them your chocolate and candy collection?"

The squat man accepted the piece of chocolate that Radha offered and he looked on interestedly as Tim unzipped his pack.

Caroline stepped unobtrusively out of the store-room. She walked casually towards Akira's room. The door was wide open. Akira's jacket hung in the same corner. His sleeping bag was rolled up and stuffed inside its cover. The rucksack was still propped near the table and on the table was the phone. Caroline unzipped her daypack, scooped up the phone, placed it in her pack, and zipped it shut. Turning, she walked out of the room.

The squat man was staring into Tim's bag. He laughed at something Dorje said. The old man guffawed and pointed at Tim. Caroline was halfway to the store-room when the sitting room door opened.

Akira stepped out.

Before he closed the door Caroline managed a peek inside. Tsering was sitting at a table looking directly at her. His large, cup-like eyes glowed as they met hers.

Caroline walked towards her friends holding her daypack in her hands. "Thank you," she said, curtseying before the squat man. "This is the pack I had left behind." Turning to Dorje she thanked him and then looking at Akira who was watching the proceedings, she thanked him too.

Akira smiled and nodded. His eyes did not register even a flicker of recognition. Akira's gaze swept past her and Caroline felt a tremor run down her spine. Akira was headed towards his room.

"Let's get out of here," she said softly to her friends and then speaking loudly she bid goodbye to the squat man. "Bye, bye sir. Thank you very much. I have to leave now. It's late and I have to walk all the way back to Leh."

Caroline strode down the stairs. She hoped Tim and Radha would follow soon. Akira could notice the missing phone any moment. Stepping out of the house, she smiled at Akira's men as she walked through the sunlit courtyard. She paused and looked back after passing through the gate. Tim had halted at the doorway and was chatting with a couple of men standing there. Radha was waiting for him in the courtyard.

"Get a move on," said Caroline loudly. "Don't stop."

Radha grabbed Tim's hand and yanked him along behind her.

Caroline hurried away. She halted by the stream and it was while she was choosing stepping-stones that an enraged cry erupted.

"Run!" she yelled.

Abandoning her search for stones she splashed through the stream. Chilly water soaked Caroline's socks and froze her feet. Reaching the far side, she pounded down the track, back towards the mouth of the valley. She glanced behind as she crossed the chortens. Tim was in front of Radha. They had crossed the stream and were running behind her. Akira was standing on the roof of the house, ranting fiercely. His men had responded to his tirade. They were rushing out of the compound in hot pursuit. Caroline's heart missed a beat. Would Akira shoot? No, it was broad daylight, she convinced herself; he could not shoot now.

Tripping on a stone, Caroline stumbled and nearly fell. "Watch out!" she screamed at herself. Akira and his gun were forgotten as she fixed her eyes on the ground. Concentrating fiercely on the uneven path she ran forward.

Helicopter At Rumbak

Lobsang spotted Raghu the moment he and Aditya stepped into the large, white tent.

"Raghu *saab*," said the Ladhaki boy running to the researcher and grabbing the lapels of his jacket. "Don't go into the village. The bad men are at Dorje's house."

Although Raghu was taken aback by Lobsang's sudden rush, he smiled. "Let's sit down and talk about it," he said. Taking Lobsang's arm he led him to one of the tables.

Aditya sat down next to them. He did not understand a word as the conversation was conducted in Ladakhi. Raghu listened intently as Lobsang related the events of the night. His eyes lit up briefly when he heard about the snow leopard encounter, but he did not pursue the subject. His questions were only about Vikram and his injury.

Raghu repeated what he had heard to Aditya.

"Is Vikram badly hurt?" enquired Aditya worriedly.

Speaking in halting Hindi, Lobsang told them about the broken bone in Vikram's leg. He told them about the impending arrival of the helicopter and Akira's plan to fly away with Tsering.

"What time is the helicopter expected?" asked Aditya.

"Just now, eight-o-clock," replied Lobsang.

Aditya's mouth popped open in dismay.

Lobsang then told them about Vikram's plan. Having no idea what a satellite phone was, the boy was not sure what Vikram's intentions were. But Aditya and Raghu comprehended instantly and they silently applauded Vikram for his thinking. Lobsang continued, bringing them up-to-date with the developments, telling them that Caroline was at this moment attempting to steal the phone.

Dorje's granddaughter served them mint tea. Her baby was fast asleep on her back. It was warm inside the tent and Aditya discarded his jacket. The tent was empty, there was no one besides them.

"Do you have a gun?" Aditya asked Raghu.

"No," smiled the bearded researcher. "I have no need for one. Some of the villagers have weapons though."

"I don't think Caroline can do the job," said Aditya speaking his mind. "If we are to save Tsering we will need guns..." Aditya halted in mid-sentence. A shadow had flashed across the tent and they heard the sound of running feet.

Caroline, flushed and breathless, skidded to a halt at the tent entrance. Her face shone with joy when she saw her camp mates.

"Raghu! Aditya!" she screamed.

She almost leapt into the tent, but caught herself at the last moment. She glanced over her shoulder and then swung her head back to look at her friends. Frenziedly unzipping her bag, she pulled out a white telephone-like instrument. Lobsang ran across to her and when he reached her side she thrust it into his hands.

"Take it," she panted. "Take the phone and make a call. Aditya! Vikram says you know whom to call."

Aditya blinked when he saw the phone, not believing his eyes. "Yippee!" he cried. "I love you, Caroline. Yes! I know just the right person to call!"

"You and Raghu handle it from here on. I've got to go. Akira's men are chasing me. You hide! Don't let them see you. I'll lead them away. They think I have the phone. Best of luck! Bye!" The girl turned and fled.

Lobsang handed the phone to Aditya.

"Move!" hissed Raghu. "Hide at the back of the tent!"

Aditya sprang into motion. Shadows appeared once more

against the tent. There was no time. Aditya hid the phone, hurriedly tucking it into his jacket.

"Help us!" cried an American voice from the entrance.

"This way," shouted Lobsang calling Aditya from behind the counter.

Aditya followed Lobsang to the back of the tent, where a cloth had been drawn behind the stove.

Tim and Radha looked pleadingly into the tent.

Shadows flashed once more and Aditya ducked behind the cloth.

"Oh no!" shouted Tim, turning and running. Radha stayed where she was.

Raghu, holding his cup of mint tea, walked out and stood beside her.

Five gasping men halted in the flattened yard outside the tent. One of them grabbed Radha and yanked her pack from her back.

"Don't do that!" protested Raghu loudly.

The cup fell from Raghu's hand as two men pounced on him.

A third man pulled out a knife.

The contents of Radha's pack were dumped on the ground. The man with the knife said something in a language that Raghu identified as Tibetan. The grip on Raghu's arms was released; Radha too was let go. Four of the five men departed, running after Tim and Caroline.

The man with the knife stepped into the tent.

Dorje's granddaughter looked worriedly at him. Aditya and Lobsang froze behind the cloth curtain.

The man's eyes darted across the tent. He stood undecided, breathing heavily. He turned finally and ran out, following his comrades.

"Aditya," called Raghu, stepping back into the tent. "Use the phone. I'll keep guard outside."

"Okay," replied Aditya from behind the curtain.

Radha heard Aditya but could not see him. "Does the

gentleman behind the curtain have the phone?" she asked when Raghu stepped back out of the tent.

Raghu did not reply immediately. Shading his eyes he stared after the running men. Three were sprinting behind Caroline and two were chasing the American boy. Caroline was in no immediate danger. She was maintaining her lead quite comfortably.

Radha repeated her question. "We helped Caroline steal the phone," she added. "I want to know whether the instrument is safe or not?"

Raghu took notice of her. "Yes, we do have the phone. Aditya, who is behind the curtain, is trying to get through now. Thank you for your help." Raghu paused, appraising Radha. "You did a good job back there, do you want to tell me what happened?"

At the back of the tent, Aditya punched in the Leh area code and followed it with Air Commodore Bhonagiri's number. It was the Air Force officer's name that sprang first to the his mind. Only he could help them in the limited time that remained. Aware that armed forces' personnel report early to work Aditya dialled the Air Commodore's direct office number.

The phone was answered at the first ring.

"Air Commodore Bhonagiri speaking," said a curt voice.

"Uncle Varun!" shouted Aditya joyfully, delighted with his luck.

"Aditya my lad! How are you? What a surprise, hearing from you. How are things?"

"Not too good I'm afraid, uncle. We need your help. Vikram and I are in trouble."

"What's wrong boy?" asked the Air Force officer, not wasting any words.

"I need a helicopter, uncle."

"What?!"

"I know the request sounds absurd, but we are in serious trouble. I am at Rumbak village, not far away – I need a machine."

"Aditya, I have 50 helicopters at my command, but I cannot despatch a single one without a good reason. What's happened? Is there an injury? Is some one hurt? Is evacuation required?"

"Vikram is hurt. He has a broken foot and is lying on a mountainside."

"Is he badly hurt?" There was concern in the Air Commodore's voice.

"He can't walk. Some of his ribs are broken too. Uncle please send the helicopter."

"Aditya, I don't think you have given me the entire story. I sense that there is something more."

"Yes, uncle there is! Another helicopter is landing here at Rumbak before eight. When it departs, it will head for the Chinese border. The helicopter is transporting a smuggler there. The smuggler is carrying goods; goods more precious than you can ever imagine. The goods are human, uncle. He is taking a young lama with him – kidnapping him to China. We have to prevent this helicopter from taking off. Trust me, uncle. This is more important than Vikram's injury. I will explain everything later. Please believe in me and despatch the helicopter."

Air Commodore Bhonagiri had been a classmate of Aditya's father. He was very close to the Khan family and although he was aware of Aditya's adventurous and rebellious nature, he was certain that Aditya was not a boy who spun absurd stories or made ridiculous demands.

He acted swiftly. "Hold the line," he said. Aditya heard him to talk to someone in the room. He heard snatches of the conversation that followed. "Group Captain Bhalla... emergency mobilisation...Rumbak..."

Aditya exulted. There was hope now. Tsering might be saved. But when Aditya looked at his watch his euphoria dissipated. Just twelve minutes remained to 8:00 a.m.

Caroline had fallen.

Raghu watched the unfortunate setback through his binoculars.

Outside Rumbak a wide river flows down a sloping glacial basin. It was either her exhaustion or the wet slippery soil under her feet that made her stumble. She fell heavily into the water and her pursuers were onto her before she could recover. The American boy had been captured too. But as Raghu suspected, the men were not interested in their captives. When they discovered that neither possessed the stolen phone, they huddled indecisively together.

Raghu guessed their next move. His fears were confirmed when they turned and started running back to the tent. They had seen Caroline halt at the tent. If the phone was not with her, the obvious place was the tent. Raghu lowered his binoculars and strode back into the tent. Pushing aside the back flap he knelt beside Aditya.

Aditya greeted him with a grin and a clenched fist salute. "I've managed to get a helicopter," he exulted.

Ignoring Aditya's jubilation, Raghu grabbed his shoulders. "Run!" he exclaimed. "The men are returning to the tent. Caroline fell. They seized her and the boy. They know the phone is not with them and they are coming back here."

Aditya reacted slowly.

Raghu shook him.

Radha entered the tent repeating what Raghu had said. "They will be here in a minute," she warned. "They are running fast."

"Oh no," breathed Aditya, realising finally that time had run out.

There was a back exit from the tent, right beside Aditya. Raghu was already kneeling, undoing its stays.

Aditya spoke urgently into the phone. "Uncle Varun, are you listening?"

The Air Commodore wasn't. Aditya could hear him reeling out instructions.

Raghu grasped Aditya by his arm and thrust him towards the exit. Aditya blinked as he emerged into the sunshine. Pausing, he pressed the phone once more to his ear. It was no use, the Air Commodore was still busy. Aditya tucked the instrument in his jacket without disconnecting it. Turning, he ran towards Rumbak village.

There were shouts from behind. Aditya looked back as he ran. The group was sprinting across the river basin towards the tent. They had seen him and one of them was gesticulating, shouting instructions to the others.

Aditya cut away from the village path. Akira was at the village and Aditya did not want to run straight into his arms. He headed for the mountains instead. Aditya wasn't worried about his pursuers. He was the fastest sprinter in his school and he was confident of staying ahead of them. But he needed to increase his lead. Distance would buy him the time to halt and resume his conversation with the Air Commodore. Aditya skirted past a field and pounded up a mountain slope. Above, there was a fold in the mountains. Aditya headed towards it.

Aditya kept glancing back as he ran. He spotted movement in the village. In the Rumbak valley, a group of people were walking between the fields. There was no time to identify them but Aditya was certain that it was Akira and his men. It was nearing eight and the helicopter would be arriving shortly. Tsering was being escorted on his final journey in Ladakh.

Aditya gritted his teeth and ran. Though he sucked air through his nostrils and gaping mouth, the oxygen entering his chest was not enough. His lungs screamed in protest and his thighs felt leaden. The fold hovered before his eyes, refusing to come closer. Aditya kept going, drawing continually ahead of his pursuers. He soon lost track of time and his vision began to blur. If he had looked back, he would have noticed that his pursuers had abandoned their chase. But Aditya did not look back. Blood pounded his ears, shutting out external sounds. He heard the thudding of his heart but he did not hear the faraway buzz of a helicopter. The fold edged closer. When his heart threatened to explode, he finally rounded the corner of the fold. Disappearing behind it he reached into his jacket and dug out the phone.

"Uncle Varun," he gasped. "Are you there?"

"What's going on?" it was the Air Commodore. There was concern in his voice. For the past few minutes all he had heard was loud breathing and the rustle of movement. "I've been calling your name over and over. What's the matter? Are you being chased?"

"Yes," panted Aditya. "I'm speaking from a stolen satellite phone. They want their instrument back."

"Good for you," chuckled the Air Commodore. "Your helicopter has taken off."

"I can see it!" cried Aditya. "There it is – across the valley."

"No Aditya. That is another helicopter you are seeing. Mine has just taken off. It is rising above the Leh airfield."

"Oh no," breathed Aditya. The machine he could see was Akira's helicopter! It had obviously appeared a while ago. His exertions had prevented him from noticing it earlier. The helicopter was sweeping across the valley, closing in on Rumbak.

"My helicopter will take time. It has to rise 20,000 feet to clear the mountains. I estimate 10 minutes to Rumbak."

Aditya stared at the approaching machine. It would be landing at Rumbak in a couple of minutes.

Akira breathed a sigh of relief when he saw the helicopter. Its appearance all but guaranteed his getaway. He had faced several ups and downs on this mission, but now he could put them all behind him.

The latest crisis was the loss of his satellite phone. Another puzzle was a boy running up a slope with his men in hot pursuit. But these niggling problems did not matter anymore. The arrival of the helicopter changed everything. He would soon be able to afford several thousand satellite phones. The boy on the slope was inconsequential.

His assignment was finally coming to an end. Only the last throw of the dice remained. Nothing mattered, except the helicopter. All he had to do was ensure that he and Tsering were safely ensconced inside the aircraft when it departed. His luck had to hold for only half an hour more – the time it would take to reach the Chinese border.

Akira's thoughts flashed ahead, anticipating possible obstacles. The pilot of the helicopter could pose a problem. The helicopter belonged to a private adventure-tourism company. The pilot had been instructed by his boss to collect his client from Rumbak and transport him to Tso Moriri. The flight plan had been cleared the previous evening when Akira had phoned and confirmed his request. Akira would have to persuade the pilot to fly beyond Tso Moriri. Akira did not consider this to be a problem. He planned to take control of the aircraft once it was airborne. Akira was carrying his gun.

Tsering was walking ahead of Akira. Four men surrounded him – two in front and two behind. The boy had been remarkably well behaved, never troubling anyone, always co-operating with his captors. Not once had Tsering betrayed any emotion, calmly accepting whatever fate held in store for him. Akira experienced a twinge of regret. It was sad that he had to abduct such an exceptional child. But Akira quickly shrugged off his moment of weakness. Business was business – nothing could ever intervene.

Akira spied the cafeteria tent when they rounded the next bend. A group of people had begun to collect around a dusty clearing. Akira looked up. The helicopter was much closer now. It was descending from a clear blue sky.

It wasn't often that a helicopter came to Rumbak. The last one had dropped by a year ago to evacuate an injured tourist. The arrival of an aircraft was always an event. Men abandoned their work, women postponed their chores and children quit their games. Villagers streamed excitedly towards the makeshift helipad. Radha, Raghu and Lobsang stood at the edge of the clearing. A few trekkers had arrived and they mingled with the rapidly collecting crowd.

Raghu could see Tsering. He was being escorted down the village path. The little boy's eyes were turned skyward as he looked up at the helicopter. There were four men around him and behind him was the Japanese kidnapper. The men who had been chasing Aditya had turned back and were also approaching the clearing.

Raghu exchanged several *jules* as the villagers arrived. He had spent many years in these mountains and was known to all the residents of Rumbak.

Tsering's eyes glowed when he saw Raghu. The look wrenched Raghu's heart. There was a wretched feeling inside him as he smiled at the boy. Raghu stamped his foot. He couldn't stand by and watch while the little lama was taken away. But no matter how deeply Raghu felt, he could not ignore the reality that stared him in the face. Four men stood in a ring around Tsering. They would soon be reinforced by the men who had been chasing Aditya. Akira was openly displaying his gun. A short, squat man with curly hair had a gun too, tucked in his belt, exhibited for all to see.

The sound of the helicopter reached deafening proportions. A turbulent wind swept the helipad kicking up a storm of dust. The machine hovered and then began its descent.

Showdown

"Aditya, my chopper is flying in the direction of Stok and gaining altitude," said the Air Commodore. The helicopter was visible from his office window. Against the solid wall of mountains on the far side of the Indus it looked like a shrunken bumblebee.

"They have to make it here in time," gasped Aditya, running as he spoke. "Is the helicopter armed?" he asked as he hurried to a place where he could look down into the valley.

"All my machines are armed, my dear boy. But I am not going to give orders to shoot."

"Uncle you have to..."

"Aditya, it is not my job to shoot down civilian aircraft. My men can radio the pilot and ask him to stay on the ground. We can issue orders and intimidate him, but nothing more. Hold on. Stay on the line, I need to talk to the pilots."

Aditya rounded the edge of the fold and looked down into the valley. He saw the crowd in the clearing. He noted with relief that his pursuers had turned around. They had abandoned the chase a considerable time ago, because they had already made it back to the tent. Aditya spotted Tsering, his guards and Akira. Raghu was there too and beside him stood Radha and Lobsang. A group of trekkers with flashy clothing had emerged from the river gorge and were hurrying towards the makeshift helipad. The approaching aircraft had panicked their pack animals and they were bolting across the open plain.

The helicopter began its descent, whipping up a cloud

of dust. The crowd shielded their eyes and backed away. Aditya turned his head, searching the wall of mountains to his left — there was no sign of the Air Force helicopter.

The shadow of the helicopter appeared in the middle of the clearing. Akira slipped on a pair of ski-goggles to protect his eyes from the dust and blade-whipped grit. He heard a sharp yell beside him and turned to look. A bearded man was grappling with his men. He had already knocked one of them down but others had jumped on him. Tsering was dangerously close to the fracas. Akira strode over and gripping the boy's shoulder pulled him away. Akira's eyes darted across the crowd searching for any further signs of trouble. Women and children were looking up in awe at the descending machine, but the village men had noticed the brawl. A flutter of anger was rippling through them.

Akira summoned his deputy, the short squat man with curly hair. The dust was making it difficult to breathe. The thunderous roar of the blades rendered conversation impossible.

A fair-skinned, dark-haired girl suddenly jumped out of the crowd, grabbing Tsering's shoulder and pulling the boy. Akira was taken by surprise and almost let go of the arm he was holding. A young Ladhaki boy ran forward and flung himself on Akira's legs. The kidnapper lost his grip on Tsering as his knees buckled. Tsering, free at last, darted towards the crowd, but the curly-haired man jumped on him. The fair-skinned girl was the same one who had stolen his telephone. She was about to tackle the curly-haired man but two burly members of Akira's team pounced on her. Angrily flinging the Ladakhi boy aside, Akira rose to his feet. Another pair of his men arrived bringing the situation under control. Akira grasped Tsering's shoulder again.

The helicopter touched down but its blades kept rotating. The dust was unbearable and the crowd backed away, widening the circle around the machine. A knot of angry villagers was collecting on one side. Akira pointed them out to his deputy. The squat man hurried in the direction of the resentful gathering. Halting some distance from them, he pulled his gun out of his belt and held it casually in his hand.

The sound level was deafening. The helicopter blades continued to swish and flurries of dust whirled beneath them. The assembled crowd was large. It had been strengthened by a group of trekkers that had just arrived. Things could easily get out of hand.

The door of the helicopter slid open revealing a man wearing dark glasses and dressed in blue pilot overalls. Handing Tsering to the custody of his men, Akira bent his head and ran forward. Wind and dust pummelled him, but the tempest eased as he neared the helicopter. Halting beneath the door he pulled out a sheet of paper from his pocket and handed it to the pilot. The paper was the receipt for the money he had paid for hiring the helicopter. As he waited, Akira spotted a second man seated at the controls of the machine. The man, dressed in red overalls, smiled at him. Akira smiled back. The pilot at the doorway returned the receipt to Akira and gestured for him to enter.

Akira turned and waved at his men. The blades continued to whisk away as Tsering, hemmed on all sides by Akira's men, was walked towards the aircraft. A tussle erupted amidst the crowd. The bearded man and the fair-skinned girl were trying desperately to break free. But his men had them under control. Akira swung his head around looking at the rest of the crowd. His deputy was standing before a sullen group of villagers with his gun pointed at them. On the far side, his other armed henchman was surveying the crowd, gun in hand.

Tsering had a calm expression on his face. He made no attempt to struggle or flee from his captors. He halted for a moment when he boarded the machine. Akira, who had seated himself, saw Tsering wave at the fair-skinned girl and the bearded man. Then bowing his head he settled himself on his seat. Akira's rucksack was placed next to Tsering. The co-pilot, in the blue suit, secured the rucksack and fastened the door. Akira tied a makeshift safety belt around Tsering. The co-pilot seated himself and waved an all-clear signal to the pilot. The helicopter shuddered and the noise intensity reached its peak as the blades whisked faster and faster. The crowd backed away again. Tsering gasped as the machine lurched off the ground.

The Air Commodore had assigned one of his officers to speak to Aditya.

"I shall be communicating with the pilots of my chopper from now on, Aditya. Squadron Leader Bhalla will talk to you in the meanwhile. Speak to him; explain everything that happens on the ground. If there is anything important, instruct him to report it to me."

Aditya relayed the events as they unfolded. He wished he was down there with his friends when he saw Raghu and Caroline hurl themselves at the kidnappers. He saw Tsering being walked forward. He choked back a sob when he saw Tsering pause and wave at Raghu and Caroline.

"Where is your machine?" cried Aditya when the door of the helicopter slid into place.

"Don't shout, young man," came the curt reply. "Have patience! These mountains are not small. The chopper has to climb to 20,000 feet to clear them. Our chopper has already crossed the snowline."

"But they have shut the door and the helicopter is about to take off."

"The AC is talking to the pilots, they have a plan. Keep a cool head, all is not lost."

A thrill of triumph surged through Akira's veins as the helicopter lifted off the ground. He was on his way. He had won! It was over, no one could not stop him now.

The ground fell away as the helicopter climbed skywards. Tsering stared down at his friends. Caroline and Raghu were still being held. They were gazing up at the machine. Tears were streaming down the American girl's face.

Akira chuckled contentedly as he looked down at the crowd. He nodded approvingly at his men below. His trusted deputy, the squat, curly-haired man would take over now. He would lead the others back across the border. They had all done a good job and Akira decided that he would compensate them well when he met them later in Tibet.

As Akira gazed downwards he got the distinct feeling that the helicopter was hovering. It was neither going up nor down. The ground below appeared stationary. Akira looked at the pilots. Both had their earphones clipped on and they seemed to be listening intently to something. Then suddenly, to Akira's horror, the machine started descending.

"What's going on?!" shouted Akira. "Why are we going down? Turn the machine around this instant! At once!"

But the pilots did not hear him. They had their earphones on and his voice was lost in the clamour of the engine.

Akira reached out and shook the co-pilot. The man half turned, signalling him to wait. There was a bump as the helicopter landed on the ground again. The co-pilot unhooked his earphones and turned.

"We have been ordered not to take off by the Indian Air Force. They have instructed us to wait till their helicopter arrives." The pilot had to shout to make himself heard.

"I am the passenger," exploded Akira. "I command you to take off."

"Sorry sir," replied the pilot. "We have to obey the Air Force."

Tsering looked on with wide eyes. He had no idea why the helicopter had returned to the ground. He saw Akira pull out his gun and point it at the pilots. The kidnapper was shouting loudly and there was a terrible expression of rage on his face.

"Get the machine off the ground! Immediately, right now!"

The pilots' faces mirrored shock as they stared at the gun.

"We have orders from..."

"I don't care who gave you the orders. Get off the ground or I shoot."

The pilots sat unmoving, looking at Akira. Their faces reflected their uncertainty.

Tsering looked at the door. If only he could open the sliding door. Tsering had seen the pilot lock the door. There was a long handle that he had slid back. Tsering thought he might be able to manage the lever. But Akira would thwart him the moment he attempted it.

"Look!" said the pilot pointing up through the bubble-shaped windscreen. "There is the Air Force helicopter."

Akira lunged for the co-pilot. Grabbing the man by the neck he jammed his gun against his forehead.

He screamed at the pilot. "Take off now or I will shoot!"

"But..."

"Now! I am counting three. I will kill your friend if you have not taken off by then."

Akira was no longer watching Tsering. The boy had already slipped off his belt. He moved towards the door.

"One!"

Tsering crouched at the door. Akira did not notice him.

"Two!"

The pilot had a look of desperation on his face. He made to say something.

"I am going to shoot NOW! Three!"

"NO!" cried the pilot. "I am taking off!" His hand moved towards the controls.

Tsering pulled at the long handle. The helicopter shuddered as it lifted off the ground. A blast of wind blew in as the door was pulled backwards. Akira turned his head.

The ground was dropping away as Tsering jumped.

"STOP HIM!" shrieked Akira, releasing the co-pilot. He lunged for the door. His legs tangled with the seats and luggage as he rolled and by the time he positioned himself for a jump, the helicopter had risen too far. It was too late to jump.

Tsering landed on the ground. Attempting to rise, he lost his footing and fell. The wind flung dust into his eyes and he could not see. The squat, curly-haired man turned away from the villagers he was guarding. Gun in hand he ran towards Tsering. The little boy rose and ran blindly. The direction he chose led him straight to the bunched group of trekkers.

There was chaos on the ground. Akira's men were all running towards Tsering. Caroline and Raghu had been released and they followed close on the heels of the kidnappers. The villagers, who had stood angrily on the side, swarmed forward.

Aditya could see the Air Force helicopter as it swooped down towards the clearing. Akira's helicopter was still ascending. There was the sound of gunfire from below. The curly-haired man was firing in the air. The crowd came to a halt.

"Tell the pilots to fire above the crowd," stuttered Aditya. "There are people down there with guns. They have to show force."

His instructions must have been relayed instantly because as the helicopter neared the crowd Aditya heard the rat-a-tat-tat of automatic fire.

The curly-haired man looked up in bewilderment. He spotted the colours of the Indian Air Force on the approaching machine. The helicopter eased its speed, positioning itself to hover above the crowd. Akira's helicopter was now far above.

The curly-haired man looked around for Tsering. But

the group of trekkers had closed ranks around him. His eyes darted amongst the crowd searching for his men. They were looking at him, waiting for instructions. There was another warning burst of gunfire from above. The curly-haired man knew then that the game was up. Gesturing to his men, he turned and ran.

Aditya erupted with joy. He couldn't believe that they had won. His eyes moistened as he saw Tsering leap into Caroline's arms. He saw Raghu and Lobsang join them. The kidnappers had grouped together and were running down the valley. Akira's helicopter was rising further into the sky.

"Well son, how was that?" The Air Commodore's voice crackled in Aditya's ear.

"Unbelievable. Fantastic. Thank you so much, Uncle Varun..." Aditya broke off, his voice choked with emotion.

"Aditya, you go join the others at the helipad. My helicopter will be landing there. The first thing I want you to do is find Vikram. Then all of you get on board and return here to Leh. There are a lot of questions you have to answer."

"Yes uncle," said Aditya, suddenly remembering Vikram.

"You can disconnect now. You must have run up a hefty bill."

"It's been taken care of, uncle. The bad guy is paying for it."

The Air Commodore laughed. "Good for you, Aditya. See you back here in Leh. Have a comfortable journey courtesy the Indian Air Force. *Jai Hind*."

The helicopter landed as Aditya ran down the mountainside. The crowd was dispersing as he sprinted towards the helipad. Caroline, Tsering and Lobsang were standing next to the machine holding hands. Raghu, Radha and Tim stood nearby. Tsering's eyes flared when he spotted Aditya. Smiling delightedly, he raised his hands above his head. Aditya raised his hands too. Tsering leapt when Aditya reached his side and the two of them energetically exchanged a high-five. Aditya blinked, holding back his tears as he hugged Tsering. Caroline looked at them laughing.

"Wow," said Tim happily.

Caroline took the phone from Aditya and held it up triumphantly. It was this diminutive instrument that had saved the day. Turning, she walked across to Tim.

"Want to make a call home, Tim?"

"You mean back home, to Seattle?"

"Yes, I do."

"Wow," Tim's eyes glowed.

"Go ahead," said Caroline handing the phone to him. "You can talk next, Radha. It's all been paid for. Right, Aditya?"

"Yes," replied Aditya. "And don't forget me, I want to call home too. I'm next in line."

Turning away Aditya walked towards the Air Force helicopter. A group of children were circling the machine, laughing and pointing at it. The pilots had stepped out and were standing at the door. Aditya halted by their side and introduced himself.

"So you are Aditya Khan," said the shorter man shaking hands. The pilot sported a neat, clipped moustache and wore dark glasses. "I'm the pilot, Squadron Leader, Shekawat and this is my partner, Flight Lieutenant, Belliappa."

Aditya shook hands with the officers.

"We have been instructed to rescue your friend and return to base," continued the Squadron Leader. "I also have orders to take you and some of your friends back to Leh with me. Are you ready?"

"Yes sir," replied Aditya. "Just give me a moment. I have to say goodbye to my friends."

"No problem," smiled Squadron Leader Shekawat.

"I knew it!" said Raghu, shaking his head after Aditya informed him about the developments. "You are planning to quit the camp. You can't even last the distance of a simple expedition like mine. You kids are all the same –

quitters! "

Aditya looked at his host in disbelief, only to see a twinkle in Raghu's eyes and a broad smile on his face.

Raghu laughed and clasped Aditya, embracing him. "You kids have performed well. It's been a great journey together. You and Vikram are welcome to join me again any time you want."

Aditya blinked. Coming from Raghu this was praise indeed.

Caroline was asked whether she wanted to return to Leh. The American girl was keen to help out with Vikram's rescue and wanted to come along. But the pilot informed her that the helicopter would not be returning to Rumbak after collecting Vikram. He told her that she would have to have to fly back to Leh with Vikram, Aditya and Tsering.

Caroline was silent for a while, undecided, wondering what to do. Vikram and Tsering were dear to her, but if she left with them she would be leaving her mother behind and she was not sure she wanted to do that. The events and the circumstances of the last few days had changed her forever. Though she wished to be with her friends, for the first time she felt a responsibility towards her mother. She experienced a parental tug that she had never felt before. It was a difficult decision but Caroline chose to stay behind.

It was decided that Tashi would fly out in the helicopter as he had sustained injuries too – probably broken bones – when he had fallen earlier with Vikram. There were no medical facilities in Rumbak and he too would receive attention at the army hospital in Leh.

Tashi was settled first at the back of the helicopter and then goodbyes were exchanged as Aditya and Tsering boarded the aircraft. Tsering requested Caroline to come along. Caroline smiled and reassured the little lama that she would meet him soon in Leh.

Raghu stopped Aditya. "You sure you want to go?" he asked. "You haven't seen a snow leopard yet."

Aditya grinned ruefully. "Don't remind me. I feel bad enough that Vikram won our bet."

"Come again, Aditya. We'll find a leopard together.'

"You bet!" said Aditya. "I'll be back."

This time there were no tears as the helicopter took off. There were only smiles as everyone waved at the departing machine. In little more than a minute they were hovering over the area where Vikram had fallen. Flight Lieutenant Belliappa spotted the injured boy almost immediately.

Landing was out of the question in the treacherous terrain. Vikram would have to be winched up while the helicopter hovered above. Aditya wanted to go down and strap up his friend but the co-pilot refused outright. Mountain rescue is a dangerous and complicated process and the Flight Lieutenant had been trained to handle the problems that could occur. Tsering and Aditya watched as the co-pilot was winched down. Working quickly he strapped Vikram in place and signalled the pilot to pull them up.

Vikram was overjoyed to see Tsering. Lying helplessly where he was, he had no idea of what had taken place. He had seen two helicopters arrive and one fly away. Vikram had feared that Tsering had been flown away. But the sight of the little lama waving down at him had brushed his doubts away forever.

The helicopter rose skywards as the Flight Lieutenant shut the rescue hatch. The Rumbak valley fell away beneath them as Vikram hugged Tsering and grinned at Aditya. Soon they were level with the snow-covered peaks. Vikram looked down as they rose above the glacier that capped Stok Kangri. He spotted the green slopes of the magical meadow. A herd of animals was running down the glacier-bound valley behind. It was a blue sheep herd. Vikram was sure that they were the same animals they had been observing the previous day. The jagged ridgeline of the mountains appeared as the helicopter moved ahead. Vikram bid a silent farewell to the magical meadow as it slipped away.

The End

The entire expedition team got to see a snow leopard. The sighting had taken place on the final evening when Caroline had detected a group of Ladakh urial, the smallest of all wild sheep, on the slopes above their camp. The sheep were high above and everyone had gathered to view them through their binoculars. Raghu sounded an alert when the urial suddenly backed off and ran towards a nearby cliff.

"There's a leopard on the mountain," he said urgently. "Search the slopes."

For ten minutes everyone scanned the slopes but to no avail. As the light was fading and when Richard had begun to mutter that the snow leopard was just a myth, Kathy screamed so loudly that everyone jumped.

"I see the leopard! I can't believe it. There he is."

The shout electrified the group and everyone trained their glasses on the area Kathy pointed out. The snow leopard's camouflage was so perfect that at first only Raghu and Tina picked out the animal. The leopard was sitting motionless beside a huge boulder close to where the urial sheep had been. It was not easy to see the animal. It was only when the boulder was pointed out to the others and they knew exactly where to look, that they saw the leopard. Raghu and Tina were delighted for their team. Their quest for the 'grey ghost' of the Himalaya had been fulfilled. There was great jubilation and back-slapping amongst the gathering. The sky turned golden in the evening twilight and they feasted their eyes on the animal till the light faded.

Though Tashi had been discharged, Vikram was still

in hospital when the expedition returned to Leh. The restfulness of a hospital bed was not what Vikram had in mind when he had planned his holiday to Leh. Luckily for him a constant stream of visitors helped relieve the tedium while he lay inert on his bed. His best friends in Leh, Dolma and Reena, dropped by everyday. *Meme* Chacko visited Vikram once before departing on one of his excursions to the Changthang. Reena's father, Air Commodore Bhonagiri stopped by often and it was he who gave them news about Akira.

The kidnapper had managed to get away, the Air Commodore regretfully informed them. Akira had commandeered his aircraft to the Chinese border after departing from Rumbak. A group of people had been waiting for him at the place he forced the pilots to land the machine. The pilots later confirmed that they saw Akira and his friends head for the border after they took off. Though the area had been searched the next day there was no trace of the kidnapper. It was concluded that he had slipped across the border into Tibet.

Aditya, Dolma and Reena updated Vikram daily with news about Tsering. The little lama sent Vikram his sincere apologies for not visiting the hospital and said that he would dearly have loved to drop by and meet his friend but given the circumstances he simply could not. Tsering was being housed at the Thikse monastery, not far from Leh. Aditya explained that although Akira was no longer a threat, a ring of security was being maintained around the boy. The team from Dharamshala, after being held up by snowbound passes, had finally arrived and they refused to let the little boy out of their sight. Not that Tsering minded, Dolma informed Vikram. The boy was being treated like a little king and was thoroughly enjoying himself.

Tsering was the only team member missing when the rest of the group assembled in Vikram's hospital room shortly after their arrival in Leh. Vikram was thrilled to hear that everyone had seen a snow leopard. Aditya, quite naturally, wasn't. But Aditya swallowed his disappointment and joined the group in a celebratory toast to their success. Another toast was raised in honour of Raghu and Tina. There was happiness and jubilation all around.

Except for Julia and Caroline everyone else was leaving on the next morning's flight. Email addresses and telephone numbers were exchanged before the group broke up. Everyone promised to stay in touch. Vikram and Aditya were invited to Singapore by Yuan Lee, to Australia by Roger, and to England by Kathy and Richard. In turn, the boys invited everybody to their homes in Delhi and their school in the Nilgiris.

Vikram was finally given permission to step out of the hospital the morning after the team split up. "Only for a few hours," the doctor warned. "I want you back after lunch." This was the moment Vikram had been waiting for. He did not care that his freedom was limited to a few hours. He was thrilled simply to be let out. Vikram had chosen to spend his free morning at the monastery visiting Tsering. Caroline and Aditya were to accompany and assist him.

Like all Tibetan monasteries, Thikse sat imposingly at the top of a hill. The road that led to the monastery climbed only half the distance to the top and a spiral of stairs led upwards from there. Vikram's right leg was encased in plaster and though he had a pair of crutches, the slope was too difficult for him to negotiate. He had to be helped and Caroline and Aditya carried him to the top. Vikram was exhausted by the time he reached the upper terraces and needed to rest for a while. Leaving Caroline with Vikram, Aditya went ahead to search for Tsering.

It was a pleasant day and the sun was shining from a clear blue sky. Vikram leaned on the terrace railing breathing heavily. Caroline stood beside him holding his crutches. The view from the top of the Thikse monastery was magnificent. The fertile Indus plain is at its widest below Thikse and row after row of green fields could be seen. The fields curved forward, following the path of the great river into the far distance. The city of Stok was visible and above it hovered the shining peak of Stok Kangri.

"Stunning, isn't it?" said Caroline.

"Wonderful," agreed Vikram.

There was silence for a while.

"Coming to India was a good decision after all?" asked Vikram.

"Yes Vikram, it was. My wish for dad is fulfilled." Caroline leaned forward on Vikram's crutches and turned her head to him. "I've been thinking of that night in the mountains, Vikram – that snow leopard sighting. I've thought several times about it and I cannot figure out how I saw the animals. The night was dark. The moon was shining, if you remember. Everything was silvery and there were only shadows. The conditions were terrible for any kind of searching. Yet I managed to spot their faint blurs. I don't believe that I could have found the animals on my own. It seems highly improbable that I could have picked them out from the mountains and shadows. Something or somebody helped me." Caroline paused and looked at the ground. "I think it was dad," she said softly. "He led me to them and then on to you."

"Maybe he did," said Vikram. "The two of you saved my life."

"You saved mine, Vikram, and I will never forget that."

A convoy of army trucks was visible far below. They looked like a child's dinky toys as they threaded their way through the fields.

"Mom and me have had long talks these last few days."

"Are you friends?" Vikram enquired.

"Yes, we are friends. We are buddies now. I'm going to live in Atlanta with her. We're going to be together. I plan to go back to school. There is an excellent university close by and though I am late I should manage to enrol for the fall semester."

"What are you going to be studying?"

"You're going to like this one." Caroline paused, bestowing a brilliant smile on Vikram. "It's going to be zoo management and wildlife sciences."

"Wow!" Vikram looked at Caroline in wonder.

"I knew you'd appreciate my choice. That's what you'd like to study, right?"

"It is! But how come you?"

"It's this trip Vikram. I've discovered that I love the outdoors. I've found out that I enjoy travelling. Wildlife sciences will give me the opportunity to travel, live outdoors and be with animals."

"It's funny how people change." Vikram shook his head. "Do you remember what you said on that mountain you tried to jump off?"

"I recall it perfectly," laughed Caroline. "People can change can't they?"

"Sometimes for the better."

"Yes, sometimes for the better."

"Wildlife sciences is not an easy subject," said Vikram. "Raghu's expedition was a five-star outing. His field trips with his students are different."

"I know; I talked to Raghu about my plans. He has warned me about how difficult it can get. He said that I would have to be tough, and willing to give up a lot in life. He gave me a long lecture, but at the end of it he told me that it is worth it."

"It is, Caroline. It is. I'm so happy for you. You better stay in touch and tell me everything."

"We'll stay in touch, Vikram."

"On email."

"Yes, and I'll be visiting too. Mom plans to come here more often. She wants to discover her roots. I'll come with her. We'll meet."

The verandah was suddenly swamped by Japanese tourists. Caroline and Vikram watched them as they chatted and posed for photographs. A curly-haired man, who looked distinctly like Akira, requested them to join in for a group photograph. The tourists collected against the railing, arranging themselves around Vikram and Caroline. The two friends placed their arms around one another and smiled for the cameraman.

Aditya arrived as the flash went off.

"Do you think that curly-haired guy is Akira?" asked Aditya after the tourists departed.

They laughed.

"Come on Vikram, Tsering's waiting for you."

Vikram followed his friends, hobbling on his crutches. Loud voices came from a prayer room. Behind the open doors were several monks sitting on the ground and chanting together. Tourists sat respectfully on one side watching them. Vikram was led through an open courtyard. Aditya halted at the far end, where there was a large wooden door. They entered a dimly-lit room. A smiling monk shut the door gently behind them.

A giant Buddha statue stood before them. Several rows of candles burned in the room and their soft light lit up the beaming face of the statue. Vikram could see that the statue was made of gold. Its serene face glinted in the candlelight. Only its head was visible. Its shoulders and chest continued down to the lower floors of the monastery. Next to the statue stood two monks. One was a senior, elderly looking man. The other was a small boy.

Vikram caught his breath. Everyone had warned him about the amazing change in Tsering's appearance. But despite the warning, Vikram couldn't help gasping at the transformed youngster who stood before him. Tsering's metamorphosis was complete. Tsering the playful, scruffy child was no more. In his place stood a neat, tidy and extremely presentable young boy. His long hair had been shaved off. His grubby, unwashed face was scrubbed clean. Gone were his T-shirt, jeans and jacket. They had been replaced by a simple robe that covered his body.

Tsering stood before them, calm and self-composed, a smile playing on his lips. "How are you Vikram?" His voice was soft and gentle and he spoke in Hindi. "I have been wanting to meet you."

"I'm fine Tsering. But who is this boy who stands before me? Where is the old Tsering I know?"

"The old Tsering is no more," said the elderly monk who stood beside the new Tsering. "The days of Tsering's previous life are over. The boy you see before you is a lama. From now on he will follow the path destiny has chosen for him. You children have helped bring him back to this path, and in doing so, you have done the Tibetan people a great service. I would like to thank you on behalf of the Dalai Lama and all his people."

The teenagers smiled and bowed their heads.

"Where will Tsering live?" asked Vikram.

"He will live at Dharamshala for the next few years. There is a lot for him to do and he has to make up for his lost years. He will study our religion there. He will be taught world affairs and he will travel extensively. He shall be groomed to be one of the leaders of his people. The little boy who stands before you has a huge responsibility on his shoulders. I do not envy him. The world we live in today is not a happy place. Our Tibetan people face great challenges and Tsering will be one of those to whom the people will look up to for direction. He has to be wise and responsible so that he can discharge the duties that destiny has chosen for him."

Vikram looked at Tsering while the monk spoke. Life had been unfair to the little boy for most of his tender years. Circumstances had changed now. He was back with his people. But life wasn't going to get any easier. It was only going to get tougher for the young lama. Vikram wondered whether Tsering truly understood his future. Tsering's new avatar — his clean and well-groomed appearance — certainly suited the task destiny had chosen for him. But in the saucer-like eyes that stared at him, Vikram could still detect the playful gleam that lurked beneath their surface. Vikram was glad to see Tsering's familiar twinkle. His scruffy face and torn clothes might be gone, but the happy exuberance still persisted. Vikram hoped that it would last forever.

Tsering stepped forward after the monk had spoken and hugged Vikram.

"Are you happy?" asked the schoolboy.

"Yes," nodded the little lama. "I am very happy." The dazzling twinkle in his eyes reflected contentment.

"I like your haircut," said Aditya.

Tsering ran his fingers over his shaven head. "You want to have haircut too? I can arrange."

"No!" exclaimed Aditya in horror.

Everyone laughed.

"I can get robes for you too," offered Tsering. "Nice, clean robes. You look like monk."

"Try making him a monk," suggested Caroline.

"Aditya? No. He can look like monk. But no become monk. Vikram, maybe..."

"No thanks," laughed Vikram.

"One day," said Tsering. "You join me one day."

"We'll see about that Tsering. You will be a big, important man then. You will be a leader. Things will be different."

"I won't be different," said Tsering.

"You won't forget about us, will you?" asked Caroline.

Tsering did not reply. He held out his hands. Vikram took one. Aditya quietly held the other. Tsering smiled, a tranquil, beautiful smile. Vikram could see the golden Buddha statue. Tsering's features mirrored its peaceful, timeless expression.

Kneeling before the boy Caroline repeated her question.

"Will you forget us?"

Tsering looked at her. "Will you try walking off a mountain again?" he asked.

"Hey..." said Caroline, colouring.

"If you do...I there to save you. I there, Vikram there, Aditya there. We all be there together. We are friends. Always..."

Afterword

Extracts from the TigerLink Newsletter regarding Shahtoosh trade.

Extracts

Poached chiru skins publicly burnt

Over **370 chiru** skins that had been recovered from poachers were **burnt to ashes** at a big public event in Xining, China. The event was aimed at raising public awareness and to reaffirm China's firm stand on the protection of endangered species. The rich 'blinded by fashion' were strongly condemned for profiting from the hunt of China's endangered animals.

Over 1100 chiru massacred

The Arjin Mountain Nature Reserve Management and the China Exploration and Research Society (CERS) mounted an expedition to **do research** on the **chiru calving sites**. At the principal site of the region it was estimated that there were approximately 15,000 females, but at the second site, what was once described as "a land full of wildlife", only 4 chiru (two male and two female) were seen. The team found that poaching was still rampant. They encountered four groups of poachers in the area and a massive chiru massacre. Two poachers were arrested and 47 pieces of chiru skin, a jeep and a rifle were confiscated. Sixty piles of chiru were found, totalling **909 bodies**. 421 of these were examined and it was found that 33% were yearling females and 28.8% were pregnant. Later **200 more chiru skins** were **confiscated** by the Ruoqiang police.

Meanwhile U.K's Vogue Magazine was reportedly extolling the virtues of shahtoosh shawls in its June issue, oblivious of the fact that they were illegal and that a species is being almost wiped out in the slaughter.

Campaign against shahtoosh

TRAFFIC has launched a **'Say no to shahtoosh' campaign**. In India the launch was held at the WWF secretariat and Ms Maneka Gandhi was chief guest. She pledged to TRAFFIC-India a shahtoosh shawl that had been presented to her on her marriage and strongly endorsed the campaign along with a number of other celebrities. Booklets, posters, stickers, badges and a video film have been produced to spread awareness of the connection between shahtoosh and the endangered chiru or Tibetan antelope.

Shahtoosh owners targeted

It seems that the message is finally being hammered home. Some of **New York's** wealthiest **women** have been **served court orders** to hand in their shahtoosh shawls and testify before a grand jury to reveal how they got them. Many well-known names from the city's `social and charitable set' are finally being forced to face the fact that their purchase and use of these garments is fuelling the annihilation of the endangered chiru or Tibetan antelope. The magazine Vanity Fair reports that the designer Valentino owns "200 shahtooshes to match every sweater, coat and suit".

A VikramAditya Story

RANTHAMBORE
Adventure

'Ranthambore Adventure' is about tigers. It is the story that is inspiring children across India to work towards saving the tiger and the country's rapidly disappearing forests.

When Aditya attempts to lay his hands on the diary of a ruthless tiger poacher, little does he know the events his actions will trigger. His ill-fated endeavour plunges Vikram and Aarti into a thrilling adventure that climaxes at the magnificent game park of Ranthambore.

'Ranthambore Adventure' also narrates the story of the tiger, Genghis. Brimming with tiger-lore, it traces the moments of Genghis's life – from his birth as a fluffy, helpless ball of fur, to his emergence as a proud and powerful predator. But vicious, greedy humans infiltrate his kingdom, seeking his skin and his bones...

A VIKRAMADITYA STORY
DEEPAK DALAL

A VikramAditya Story

LADAKH
Adventure

Ladakh is the land beyond the Himalayas. On a visit to this remote, majestic outpost of India, Vikram and Aditya camp out on the lofty Changthang Plateau. Here, they meet a young Tibetan boy named Tsering.

But Tsering is unexpectedly abducted and Aditya pulls off a daring rescue. Suddenly Vikram and Aditya are on the run. On the frozen plateau, often referred to as the 'Roof of the World', the two friends play a dangerous game of hide-and-seek with a band of mysterious men.

Who is Tsering? Why is he being chased with such fierce resolve? Discover the fascinating secret of Tsering in this fast-moving adventure tale.

'Ladakh Adventure' is another enthralling VikramAditya story, set in a wondrous land of startling contrasts and magnificent mountains.